Have you got all of Enid Blyton's FAMOUS FIVE books?

(*Also available as dramatised recordings on CD)

ADVENTURE GAME BOOK 5

Join the Famous Five on their adventure in horse-drawn caravans and make friends with a boy from the circus and his clever pet chimp. Find out why some sinister people want to ruin their camp. You can choose a pathway for the Five – but will you solve the mystery and catch the crooks or will you take a false trail along the way?

This exciting game story is based on Enid Blyton's *Five Go Off In A Caravan*.

Enid Blyton

THE FAMOUS FIVE

ADVENTURE GAME BOOK 5

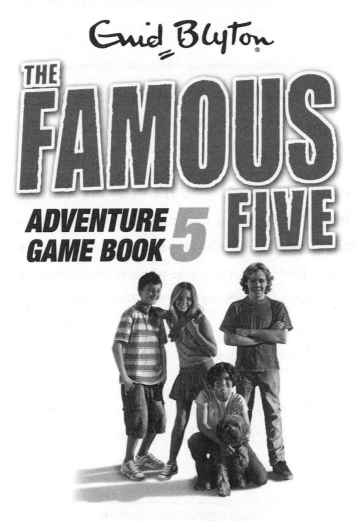

**An Enid Blyton story devised
and adapted by Mary Danby**

Illustrated by Kate Rogers

*Hodder
Children's
Books*

A division of Hachette Children's Books

THE FAMOUS FIVE

Adventure Game Book

Unlike an ordinary book, which you can read straight through from beginning to end, this is a game book, in which *you* choose how the story should go.

Begin at section number **1**. At the end of each section you are told which section to read next. Sometimes you will find you have a choice. (For instance, at the end of section 7 you have to decide whether or not George should make a telephone call to her mother.)

Every time you have a choice to make, there will be one way that is the quickest and best – and you have to guess (or work out, if you can) which it is. If you choose the wrong number, you can still carry on reading, but when you find yourself back at the main story you will find you have picked up a few 'red herrings'.

A red herring is the name given to something

that carries you away from the main subject (as when someone is telling you a story and puts in all sorts of details that don't really matter). Your aim is to try and stay on the main track, without going off down the little side roads.

See if you can make the right choices and find your way to the end of the story without picking up too many red herrings. Red herrings are represented in the text by a symbol: $\bigcirc\!\!\triangleleft$. (Use a pencil and paper to add up your score as you go along.) Then turn to the back of the book to see how well the Famous Five (and you) have done.

1

'I love the beginning of the summer holidays,' said Julian. 'They always seem to stretch ahead for ages!'

Julian, Dick, George and Anne were lying in a

sunny garden during the first week of the summer holidays. Beside George lay her big black and white dog, Timmy, who went everywhere with her. Usually George and her three cousins spent their summer holiday at George's house by the sea, but this time, for a change, they were all at the home of Julian, Dick, and Anne.

'Dad said this morning that if we didn't want to stay here this holiday we could choose what we wanted to do,' said Anne. 'Has anyone got any ideas?'

'Yes,' said Dick, who was sometimes a bit lazy, 'I'd like to sleep most of the time!'

Go to **7**.

2

'We're off for a rest,' said the boy. 'Up in the hills, near a lake.'

'Which is your caravan?' asked Dick.

'That one,' said the boy, pointing to a gaily painted caravan that was going past. 'I live with my Uncle Dan, who's the chief clown in the circus.'

The children all stared at the man driving the caravan. He looked really bad-tempered, and it was hard to imagine him making a single joke.

'I must go,' said the boy. 'Nice to meet you. My name's Ned, by the way.'

Ned ran after the caravan and jumped nimbly in. The children watched the rest of the circus go past. There were monkeys, a string of horses, and a chimpanzee.

'Well, I suppose we'd better go and have tea,' said Julian. 'Come on!'

'Wait a minute,' said George. 'Where's Timmy?'

If you think Timmy is chasing after the circus, go to **8**.
If not, go to **14**.

'Just think,' said George, ignoring Dick, 'if we went to Kirrin we could camp in that field at the back of our house. Mum could give us supplies, and we could probably use the kitchen for washing up.'

'Oh, *George*,' groaned Dick. 'The whole idea of going off in the caravans is to look after ourselves, do things like buying food from farmhouses, and washing up in streams. If we camp behind your house, the first thing we know Aunt Fanny will be making us have baths every night!'

'We all love going to Kirrin, George,' said Julian, 'you know we do, but it would be nice to do something different, wouldn't it?'

Go to **19**.

The other three lay in the sun and thought about going to Kirrin Cottage. It was a wonderful place to be in hot weather, because they could spend all day on the beach, and swim as much as they liked. There was a pool in the nearest town to their home, but dogs were not allowed in, and George wouldn't leave Timmy behind.

Just then George came back. She flopped down on the lawn beside Anne and shook her head.

'I'm afraid it's no good,' she said. 'Mum says that they're having all the bedrooms painted, and there's nowhere for us to sleep.'

The other three groaned.

'Well, we'll have to think of something else,' said Dick. 'Anyone got any ideas?'

There were sleepy grunts from the others, but nobody said anything, and before long they had all dozed off, except Timmy. Since all the others were asleep, he considered himself to be on guard.

Go to **9**.

5

The following day the milkman brought his black horse to the house, and the two horses were harnessed to the caravans. Julian climbed up on the front of the green caravan, while George drove the red one. Dick sat beside Julian, and Anne was with George. Timmy sat on the other side of George with his tongue hanging out, swishing his tail with excitement. The four children were all grinning happily.

'Goodbye, Mum!' shouted Anne. 'We're off on another adventure!'

Go to **16**.

'Doesn't it look exciting?' said George. 'I wish I belonged to a circus that went wandering all over the place.'

'Fat lot of good you'd be in the circus,' said Dick rudely. 'You can't even turn a cartwheel.'

He pointed to a boy who was turning cartwheels very quickly, going over and over on his hands and feet, turning himself like a wheel. It looked very easy, but Dick knew it wasn't.

'I wish I could do that,' said Anne in admiration.

The boy came up to them and grinned. He had two terrier dogs with him. Timmy growled, so George put her hand on his collar.

'Don't come too near,' she warned. 'Timmy isn't quite sure about you.'

'We won't hurt him!' said the boy, and grinned again. He had a freckled face and a shock of untidy hair. The boy clicked his fingers and the two dogs rose at once on their hind legs and walked behind him with funny little steps.

'Are they performing dogs?' asked Anne. 'Are they yours?'

'These two are,' said the boy. 'This is Barker and this is Growler. I've had them since they were puppies.'

'Where are you giving your next show?' asked George eagerly. 'We'd like to see it.'

Go to **2**.

7

George looked at Dick scornfully. 'Imagine wanting to sleep through all this lovely weather,' she said. 'Timmy and I want to spend as much time as possible out of doors, don't we, Timmy?'

'Woof!' said Timmy in agreement, and the others all laughed.

George spent so much time outside that she was permanently tanned, and with her curly hair cut short she looked like the boy she would have liked to be. Her real name was Georgina, but everyone called her George.

'I know,' said Anne. 'Let's go to your parents' house at Kirrin for a fortnight!'

'That sounds like a good idea,' said Dick. 'What do you think, George? Why not phone your mother and ask?'

If you think George should ring her mother, go to **12**.
If not, go to **17**.

8

They all looked round the garden, but there was no sign of Timmy.

George whistled for him, but nothing happened.

'I wonder where he's gone?' said Anne. 'It's not like him to wander off, is it?'

'No,' said George, who was beginning to look a

bit worried, 'it's not.'

'Wait a minute,' said Dick, 'do you suppose he might have gone after the circus? He was very interested in all the strange animals, wasn't he?'

George turned and ran back down the drive to the gate. She opened it and went out into the road to see if the circus was still in sight.

Go to **18**.

9

If you have arrived from **4**, *score one red herring:* ⌒.

The garden sloped up a hillside. From where he sat, Timmy could see quite a long way, both up and down the road that ran by the house. He heard a dog barking in the distance, and his ears twitched in that direction. He heard people walking down the road, and his ears twitched again. He missed nothing, not even the robin that flew down to get a caterpillar on a bush not far off.

Suddenly he sat up and sniffed. He could smell something different, something he didn't recognise. He sniffed again. No – he was mistaken. All he could smell were the usual smells – grass and sheep and people – all things that he knew well. He lay down again and rolled over on his side. He was just settling himself more comfortably when something made him sit up. He could hear a strange rumbling noise, as if something heavy was coming along the lane, and he could smell horses.

Timmy had seen brewers' wagons drawn by shire horses going up and down the lane from time to time – there was a brewery on the outskirts of the nearest town. Could he hear one of them now? Or was it something else?

If you think it's a brewer's wagon, go to **15**.
If you think it's something else, go to **20**.

At last the great day came when the two caravans trundled up the drive. The children's mother had borrowed them from an old friend. They were not painted quite like the circus caravans, but were a little more modern. One was red, with green curtains, and the other was green with red curtains. The four children were absolutely thrilled, and in no time at all were exploring inside both vans.

'Bunks along one side – is that where we sleep? Brilliant!' shouted Dick.

'There's a proper stove to cook on, but I vote we cook outside on a camp fire. Look at the bright frying pans and all the cups and saucers hanging up!' said Anne.

They were all longing to set out at once, but the second horse would not be arriving until the following day. His name was Trotter, and he belonged to the local milkman. All the children learnt riding at school, and would have no trouble looking after the two horses properly. They spent the rest of the day filling the caravans with all the things they would need. Julian's father had given him a useful little book with the names of farmers who allowed people to park caravans in their fields.

'You must always choose a field where there is a stream if you can,' said their father. 'Dobby and Trotter will need fresh water.'

Go to **5**.

11

The loud barking woke all the children at once. George sat up and saw the circus procession. She gave a yell.

'Hey, everybody! There's a circus procession going by. Look!'

They all sat up, wide awake now, and stared at the caravans going slowly down the road.

'Let's go down to the gate and have a closer look,' suggested Dick.

They all got up and ran down the garden into the drive that led to the road. The procession was just passing the gate. It was a marvellous sight. The caravans were painted in bright colours, and little flowery curtains hung at the windows. At the front of each caravan sat the man or woman who owned it, driving the horse that pulled it. Only the front caravan was pulled by an elephant.

Go to **6**.

12

George lay back and squinted up at the sky while she considered the idea of going to Kirrin Cottage. Being at Kirrin meant being able to swim every day, go out in her boat and, above all, visit her beloved Kirrin Island. The only disadvantage was that her father might have started an experiment, and need plenty of peace and quiet, which he couldn't have with four children and a dog in the house! George's father was a scientist, a very clever man, but he was apt to be short-tempered when he was working. Still, the idea of being able to swim as much as they liked in the very hot weather was tempting.

George got to her feet. 'I'll go and ring Mum,' she said, 'and see what she thinks.'

Go to **4**.

13

When the children's father came home that evening he listened carefully to what they had to say, then thought for a moment.

'Well,' he said. 'As it happens I have to go up north on business for ten days, and I would like your mother to come with me. I think you are sensible enough to look after yourselves for a few days – it will do you good. So you *can* go, but you'll need two caravans, not just one. Our old horse Dobby can pull one of them, and I'll see if we can borrow another horse for the other caravan.'

'Where can we get the caravans?' asked Julian.

'We can hire them,' replied his father. 'There are several firms that hire out caravans, or we may even be able to borrow *them*, too, if we're lucky.'

The children were absolutely delighted. It sounded almost too good to be true – sleeping in bunks, cooking meals in the open air, being able to wander wherever they liked.

'Well,' said Julian. 'Where are we going to go?'

'I vote we go down to Kirrin,' said George, who was longing to visit her precious island. 'We can live in the caravans and not bother Mother and Father at all.'

'I'd like to go up to the hills for a change,' said Dick.

If you like George's idea, go to **3**.
If you prefer Dick's, go to **19**.

George looked up the garden to the house, and at that moment she felt a wet nose against her hand.

'Oh, there you are, Timmy,' she said. 'I thought we'd lost you. Come on – we'd better go back to the house and have tea.'

The five of them walked back to the house.

'Hello, Mum. Did you hear the circus go by?' asked Anne, as her mother came out of the kitchen. 'Wasn't it exciting!'

Go to **22**.

15

Timmy stood up and walked down the lawn towards the gate, but as he went he saw one of the big brewers' wagons going past. So that was what he had heard! It was a very large wagon, stacked with barrels, and the two horses that drew it were huge, gleaming animals with magnificent feathery feet. Timmy trotted back to where the children lay asleep in the sun and sat down again. He was getting rather tired of waiting for them to wake up.

After a while he realised that the noise from the road didn't seem to be fading. Perhaps there was something else coming.

Go to **20**.

Go to **20**.

16

The two caravans moved slowly down the drive and into the road at the bottom. Julian was so happy that he sang at the top of his voice, and the others joined in. Dobby plodded on slowly, enjoying the sunshine and the fresh air. Trotter followed at a short distance. He was very interested in Timmy, and always turned his head when the dog barked or got down for a run.

It had been decided that they should make their way to the hills where they hoped to find the circus, and before they had been travelling for more than a few minutes they came to a place where the road forked. Julian pulled Dobby to a halt and reached for the map, to see which fork they should take. He was just unfolding it when a car came down the right-hand fork and stopped. The driver stared hard at the two caravans.

'He's winding down the window,' said Dick. 'I wonder if he wants to speak to us?'

*If you think the driver of the car speaks to them, go to **21**.*
*If you think he doesn't, go to **27**.*

17

'No point,' said George at once. 'I went home at half term, and Mum said that Dad was just beginning one of his experiments in something or other – and you know what that means. If we go there we'd have to walk about on tiptoe, and talk in whispers, and keep out of his way all the time.'

'Well, that's out,' said Julian. 'But what shall we do then, stay here?'

There were lazy murmurs from the others, who were all lying on their backs with their eyes closed, and before long they were all asleep, except

Timmy, who regarded it as his duty to stay awake and guard them.

Go to **9**.

18

There was no sign of the circus, but the procession was so slow-moving that George knew she could catch up with it if she ran. She dashed down the road to the corner, and there was the end of the procession, rolling slowly along in the sunshine.

George ran on, calling Timmy's name. It didn't take her long to reach the last caravan as it ambled along.

'Have you seen my dog?' she shouted at the woman driving the caravan.

'What does he look like?' asked the woman.

'He's a big black and white dog with a friendly face,' replied George.

'Oh yes,' said the woman. 'I saw him a moment

ago, running up the road beside the chimp. Seemed very interested in the chimp, he did.'

'Thank you,' called George, and on she went.

Go to **25**.

19

If you have arrived from **3**, *score* ⌒.

George looked mutinous for a moment, then she smiled.

'All right,' she said, 'let's go up to the hills. After all, we've spent a lot of time on Kirrin Island. It would be nice to do something different.'

'We could go and camp near the circus!' exclaimed Julian. 'That boy Ned said they were going to camp in the hills near a lake, didn't he? If we're near the lake, we can swim, and we'd be able to see all the circus animals, and maybe make friends with some of the people there. How long do you think it will be before the caravans get here, Mum?'

'Oh, three or four days,' said their mother, 'but you'll need plenty of time to get everything ready. Now off you all go to bed.'

The four of them went upstairs, chattering excitedly about all the things they would need for their holiday. They could hardly wait for the caravans to arrive!

Go to **10**.

20

If you have arrived from **15**, *score one red herring:* ⌒ᗡ.

He got up and went to the gate to look down the lane. Something was coming along the road, something that made Timmy shake with excitement. A big procession came winding up the road, with a rumble and a clatter of wheels – a slow procession, headed by a very strange thing.

Timmy had no idea what it was that headed the procession. Actually, it was an elephant, and Timmy smelt its smell, strange and strong, and didn't like it. He smelt the scent of the monkeys in their travelling van, too, and he heard the barking of the performing dogs in their van. He answered them defiantly. 'WOOF, WOOF, WOOF!'

Go to **11**.

21

The car pulled over beside the caravan, and the driver looked up at the two boys. He had hair so fair that it looked almost white, and chilly blue eyes. He smiled at them.

'Is this the right road for the village?' he asked.

'Yes,' replied Julian politely. 'The village is about five miles from here.'

'Thank you,' said the man, and he smiled again.

There was something about his smile that neither Julian nor Dick liked very much. He smiled only with his mouth, not with his eyes, and he stared hard at them both. Julian gathered up the reins, waiting for the man to drive away, but he didn't move!

Go to **28**.

22

If you have arrived from **25**, *score* ⌒ ⌒ .

The four children ran upstairs to wash their hands for tea. George was just picking up the towel when she suddenly stood still and looked at the others.

'Listen!' she said. 'I've had the most fantastic idea. Why don't we all go off in a caravan this holiday?'

'George!' shouted Anne. 'What an amazing idea! Do you think we'll be allowed to go off on our own?'

'Why not?' said George. 'We've proved that we can be sensible and good at looking after ourselves in some of our other adventures. Come on, let's go and ask!'

They tore downstairs and into the dining-room.

'Mum!' cried Dick. 'George has had the most fantastic idea! She suggested that we go off in a caravan for a while. *Please* say we can.'

'Goodness,' said his mother. 'I think I'd better talk to your father before I say yes or no. You'll have to wait until he comes in.'

Go to **13**.

23

The man stared coldly at them for a moment before driving on down the road.

'I think you offended him,' said Dick. 'He was only trying to be friendly.'

'Where we're going is none of his business,' said

Julian. 'You shouldn't get into conversation with strangers. In any case, there was something about him I didn't like. Not one little bit.'

Go to **26**.

24

Towards evening they began to think about where they were going to camp for the night.

'We must keep our eyes open for a farm,' said Julian. 'I'll look in the book and see if there's one nearby.' He studied the book for a moment, then looked up. 'There's a farm quite close to here,' he said. 'With any luck we shall be able to buy some bacon and eggs and stuff for breakfast from the farmer's wife when we go and ask permission to camp.'

The horses plodded on for another mile before Dick gave a shout.

'Look!' he called. 'I can see the farmhouse!'

Sure enough, there was a cluster of barns and outhouses, and a rather run-down-looking farmhouse. It was set quite a long way back from the road, and they would not have been able to see it over the hedge if they had not been high up on the seats of the caravans.

'There's another farmhouse on this side of the road,' exclaimed Anne, who had sharp eyes. 'Look, up the road there.'

They all craned their necks, and could just see another group of farm buildings, right on the road.

'I wonder which one is the one we want,' said George.

If you think they should try the farmhouse set back from the road, go to **29**.

If you think they should go to the one further up the road, go to **35**.

A bit further up the road George saw Timmy. He was gambolling along in the road, dancing round and round the chimp's trailer. The chimp was awake now, and looking rather puzzled by his excited visitor.

'Timmy!' called George. 'Come here at once!'

Timmy turned and saw George. He gave a longing look at the chimp, as if wondering why his new friend wouldn't come down and play with him, then he trotted obediently back to George, and they went back to the house. The other three were waiting at the gate.

'Come on,' said Dick impatiently. 'Mum called us in for tea five minutes ago!'

The five of them walked up the garden and into the house.

'Hello, Mum. Did you hear the circus go by?' asked Anne, as her mother came out of the kitchen. 'Wasn't it exciting!'

Go to **22**.

26

Julian passed the reins to Dick and jumped down to the road.

'I'm just going to tell George and Anne what that was all about,' he said. 'They'll be wondering why we were talking to that man, and they ought to know that we didn't like the look of him.'

He ran back and quickly told the girls, then he jumped up on the driving seat once more and took the reins from Dick.

'Now, we take the left fork here,' he said, and the two caravans moved on.

Go to **30**.

As the children watched, the driver of the car flicked an apple core out of the window, and wound it up again. Then he drove on without looking at the two caravans.

'It's rather messy of him to drop apple cores in the road,' said Dick.

'Oh, some bird or animal will eat it, I guess,' replied Julian. 'Now, we take the left fork here, according to the map.'

He shook the reins, and Dobby moved on.

Go to **30**.

28

'Tell me,' said the man, 'are you heading for the hills? You have chosen a very pleasant way to travel.'

'Yes,' answered Dick. 'We're with the two girls in the caravan behind us.'

'Girls!' exclaimed the man. 'I thought one was a boy.'

'No,' said Dick with a grin. 'She just wishes she was one.'

'I suppose you're going to the lake, aren't you?' asked the man, with another of his cold smiles.

'Well, we—' began Dick, but Julian interrupted him.

'I don't want to seem rude, but I think we should be getting along now.' He clicked at Dobby, and the caravan moved forward.

Go to **23**.

29

'I think we should try the nearest one,' said Dick. 'I'm getting very hungry, aren't you, Julian?'

Julian laughed. 'You're always hungry!' he said. 'But I think it'd be a good idea to try this farm first, and then we can go on to the other one if need be.'

Julian guided Dobby carefully into the narrow lane that led up to the farmhouse. George followed him with Trotter. The lane was quite long, but eventually they found themselves in a rather dirty cluttered farmyard.

'I don't much like the look of this,' said Julian. 'It doesn't look like a very well-run farm.'

Go to **32**.

30

If you have arrived from **26**, *score* ◁ ◁ ◁.

For the rest of the day the two caravans ambled peacefully down the quiet country lanes. They stopped for lunch at about half past twelve, and ate a huge picnic while the two horses munched away at some juicy grass in a ditch. After they had picnicked they set off again. Dick took his turn at driving Dobby, while Julian walked beside the caravan to stretch his legs. Timmy jumped down from his seat beside George and ran along with Julian for a while.

They covered quite a distance that day, though Anne was disappointed that they didn't reach the hills where the circus was camping.

'We won't reach the hills for four or five days,' said Julian. 'They're miles away!'

Go to **24**.

31

The farmer was not in, but the farmer's wife gave them permission to spend the night in the field by the stream.

'I can see you won't leave litter, or go chasing the farm animals,' she said. 'I've got plenty of new-laid eggs, and you can have some of the plums off that tree over there too.'

Julian said it was too hot to cook in the caravans,

so he built a fire in the field, and Anne cooked eggs and bacon and fried bread for them all. They lingered over the little camp fire for a long time, but eventually they decided that it was time for bed. They were all looking forward to sleeping in the little bunks.

Go to **38**.

32

Julian passed the reins to Dick and jumped down from his seat. He walked over to the front door of the farmhouse and rang the bell. In the distance he could hear several dogs barking, but no one came to the door. He rang again, and waited, but still nothing happened. He was just turning away from the door when suddenly it was opened. A small, rather dirty-looking man stood there, scowling at Julian.

'What do you want?' he snapped.

'We were wondering if you would let us park our caravans in one of your fields overnight,' said Julian politely. 'We would also like to buy some butter and eggs and bacon, if you have any to sell.'

'Go away,' said the man violently. 'I never let anyone camp on my farm. Now get out of here, or I'll call the police!'

He slammed the door in Julian's face. The boy climbed back on to the seat of the caravan and took the reins from Dick.

'What a charmer!' he said. 'Never mind, we'll go on and try the other farm.'

They went back down the lane into the road.

Go to **35**.

33

'What gorgeous fun to come down here every day and swim,' said Dick. 'I think Timmy's enjoying the swimming as much as we are, George.'

They decided to have a picnic by the lake, and to set the horses free to have a swim if they wanted one. But all they wanted was to drink and to stand knee-high in the water, swishing their tails to keep away the flies.

'Where's the circus camp?' said George, as they sat munching ham and tomato sandwiches. 'I can't see it.'

Go to **41**.

34

Just then Julian came running up to see why George had stopped.

'What's the matter?' he asked.

'There's no bridge over the stream,' said George. 'Could you look at the map and see if there's one nearby, please?'

Julian went back to the other caravan and got

the map. He brought it over to where George was waiting.

'Yes,' he said, 'there's one a bit further upstream. If we turn along the bank, we'll come to a road with a bridge over the stream. It's not very far away.'

It was rather bumpy, driving along the bank, but after about half a mile they came to a main road and, looking to their left, saw a bridge humping over the stream. Both caravans crossed over, and a few hundred metres further on they saw a wide path leading to the edge of the lake.

'This must be the path that the circus people used,' said George, turning down it. 'I can see, heavy ruts that must have been made by the animal trailers.'

Sure enough, when they reached the lakeside, there was the circus camp only a short distance away.

Go to **46**.

35

If you have arrived from **32**, *score* ◁ ◁.

'What's the name of the farm in your book, Julian?' asked George.

'It's called Longman's Farm,' said Julian. 'There should be a stream nearby, according to this map. If we could camp there, it would be perfect.'

'Well, this farm is called Coldharbour Farm,' said

Anne, pointing at a battered board at the end of the lane, which none of them had noticed before.

'It's obvious that this isn't the place in the book, then,' replied Julian. 'Come on, we'll try the farm further up the road.'

Longman's Farm was a pleasant, red-roofed building, glowing in the evening sun. Hens clucked about in the yard, and one or two dogs watched their arrival. Julian rang the bell.

Go to **31**.

36

They all looked out for the hills next day as the caravans rumbled slowly down the lanes, and in the afternoon they saw them, blue in the distance.

'There they are!' said Julian. 'The Merran Hills – and Merran Lake must lie at the foot. There should be a brilliant view over it if we can get high enough.'

The hills came nearer and nearer. They were quite high, and looked lovely in the evening light.

'We won't have time to climb them and find a camp site tonight,' said Julian, looking at his watch. 'We'd better make camp near here this evening, and then make our way up to the hills tomorrow morning.'

'Oh no,' said Dick, 'I think we should press on to the hills tonight.'

If you think they should camp where they are, go to **42**.
If you think they should drive on, go to **47**.

37

They had not gone far the next morning before George caught sight of something flashing blue between the trees.

'Look! There's the lake! Merran Lake!' she shouted. 'Make Dobby go more quickly, Julian! I'm longing to come out in the open and see the lake!'

Soon the lane became a broad cart track that led over a heathery common. The common sloped right down to the edge of an enormous lake that lay glittering in the August sunshine.

'It's lovely!' cried Anne, jumping down from the driving seat of the red caravan. 'Let's go swimming right now!'

'Yes, let's,' said Julian, and they all rushed into their caravans, stripped off jeans and shirts and pulled on swimming things. Then they tore down to the lakeside and plunged into the water.

It was very warm at the edge of the water, but further in, where it was deep, the lake was deliciously cold. All the children could swim strongly, and they splashed and yelled in delight.

Go to **33**.

The four children climbed into the two caravans after washing in the stream. They undressed and got into the bunks. It was too hot for blankets; all they needed was a sheet over them.

At first Anne tried sleeping in the lower bunk, but Timmy kept trying to climb up to get to George. He wanted to lie on her feet as usual. Anne got cross.

'George! You'd better change places with me. Timmy keeps jumping on me, and I'll never get to sleep.'

The two girls changed places, and soon they were both sound asleep, with Timmy curled up on George's feet, as usual. They slept soundly, tired after their long day in the fresh air.

Far into the night Anne suddenly woke with a jump. She lay still for a moment, wondering what had woken her up. Then suddenly there was a bump, and the caravan shook! Timmy barked, and both Anne and George nearly fell out of their bunks in fright! Was something trying to get in?

'Perhaps one of the horses is bumping against the caravan,' whispered Anne.

'Or it might be a farm animal straying,' answered George.

If you think it was one of the horses, go to **48**.
If you think it was a farm animal, go to **43**.

39

George moved Trotter to the edge of the stream to have a closer look. The banks were quite steep further upstream, but flattened out towards the lake, so that the level of the water was only a few inches below the bank.

'What do you think, George?' asked Anne. 'Can we ford it?'

'I think I'd better get down and see how deep the stream is before we try,' said George. 'Here, Anne, hold the reins a minute.'

Anne took the reins from George, who swung herself down to the ground. She walked over to the stream, and knelt down on the bank.

Go to **49**.

40

The next three or four days were absolutely perfect, with blue skies, blazing sun, and two wonderful caravans. Anne had almost forgotten that they were heading for the hills to find the circus camp. She was quite happy ambling along the country lanes. The others were all enjoying themselves too.

That night, when they stopped, Julian got out the map.

'We're just here,' he said, pointing to a place on the map. 'It looks as if we ought to come to those hills tomorrow, and maybe find the circus.'

'Good!' said Dick. 'I hope Ned will be there. I'm sure he'll show us round the camp if we ask him.'

Go to **36**.

41

The children looked all around the edge of the lake, which stretched as far as the eye could see. At last Anne's sharp eyes spied a small spire of smoke rising in the air about a mile or so round the side of the lake.

'The camp must be in that dip at the foot of the hills over there,' she said. 'I guess the road leads round to it. We'll go that way, shall we, and go up to the hills behind the camp?'

'Yes,' agreed Julian. 'We'll have plenty of time to have a word with Ned, and to find a good camping place before nightfall – and to find a farm, too, that will let us have food. Won't Ned be surprised to see us?'

They cleared up, harnessed the horses again, and set off for the circus camp. Now for a bit of excitement!

Go to **44.**

42

If you have arrived from **45**, *score* ◯ ◯ ◯ ◯.
If you have arrived from **53**, *score* ◯ ◯ ◯ ◯ ◯.

'No,' said Julian firmly. 'We'll have to stop for the night soon. According to the book there's a farm a short way up the road. We'll see if we can stay there.'

They came to the farm, which was set by a wide stream that ran along swiftly. Julian got permission to camp from the farmer's daughter, who also sold him milk, butter, eggs and bacon, and a little crock of yellow cream. She also offered them raspberries from the garden if they liked to pick them.

'Thanks. That's very kind,' said Julian. 'Could you tell me if there's a circus camping up in the hills?'

'Yes, I think there is,' replied the farmer's daughter. 'I saw the procession go by about a week ago.'

The two boys said goodbye to her and went back to the caravans. The next morning they set off on what they hoped would be the last lap of their journey. They would find a lovely camping place and stay there until it was time to go home.

Go to **37.**

43

'I think I'd better get up and see what it is,' said George, and she climbed out of her bunk and picked up her torch. She opened the door of the caravan and looked out, flashing her torch around, but there was nothing unusual to be seen. Suddenly the caravan gave another lurch. George jumped to the ground and walked round the caravan, holding her torch in front of her.

Anne sat up in her bunk, straining her ears for any sound from George. She was half afraid that it might be a tramp who was wandering around. Just then George climbed back into the caravan and got back in her bunk.

'What was it?' asked Anne apprehensively.

George chuckled. 'It was a cow,' she answered. 'It had got out of the next field, so I took it back and closed the gate. Now let's go back to sleep!'

The two girls were drifting comfortably to sleep when suddenly something bumped the caravan again.

Go to **48**.

The two caravans set off again towards the circus camp. As they got closer, they could see that it was in a comfortable hollow, set at the foot of the hills – a quiet spot, well away from any houses, where the animals could enjoy a certain amount of freedom and be exercised in peace.

George was in front, for a change, and suddenly she pulled Trotter to a halt.

'Oh, bother!' she exclaimed.

'What's the matter?' asked Anne.

George pointed ahead. 'I think that's a stream, and if it is, how are we going to get across? There doesn't seem to be a bridge in sight.'

'Perhaps we should try to find a bridge,' suggested Anne.

'I think it would be quicker if we tried to ford the stream,' argued George.

If you think they should try to find a bridge, go to **34**.
If you think they should try to ford the stream, go to **39**.

Dick and George made their way steadily through the wood, from time to time calling the horses' names.

Suddenly, George stopped. 'Listen!' she said.

In the quiet of the wood they both heard munching sounds coming from their right. They walked around a clump of trees, and there were the horses, standing in a small clearing, happily cropping a patch of grass.

George caught Dobby's rope, while Dick grabbed Trotter's, and they led them firmly out of the wood.

'Hey! Julian! Anne!' called Dick. 'We've found the horses!'

The other two saw Dick waving and came running up, and in no time at all the two runaway horses were safely harnessed to the caravans again.

'Have we still got time to get to the hills this evening?' asked Anne.

Go to **42**.

46

If you have arrived from 56, score ᑕᑕ ᑕᑕ ᑕᑕ.

The circus caravans were set round in a wide circle. Tents had been put up here and there. The big elephant was tied to a stout tree. Dogs ran about everywhere, and a string of shining horses was being paraded round a large field nearby.

The children looked at everything with interest as their caravans came nearer to the circus camp. Few people seemed to be about that hot afternoon.

'There they all are!' exclaimed Anne, standing up on the driving seat to see better. 'Look, the chimpanzee is loose, isn't he? No, he isn't – someone has got him on a lead. Is it Ned with him?'

'Yes, it is,' said Julian. 'Fancy walking about with a live chimp like that!'

Go to 50.

'I think we'd better ask the other two what they think,' said Julian, pulling on the reins to halt Dobby. 'You hold on to Dobby, Dick, and I'll go back and have a word with the girls.'

He handed the reins to Dick and jumped down. Running back to where the second caravan had stopped, he explained to Anne and George that Dick wanted to go on, but he thought they should stop where they were for the night.

The two girls looked at each other.

'Let's go on to the hills,' said George. 'I'm longing to see the circus again.'

'Me, too,' said Anne.

'All right,' said Julian. 'I'll tell Dick.'

Go to **51**.

*If you have arrived from **43**, score ⌒.*

George rolled out of her bunk and opened the door. Timmy shot out and started barking at the top of his voice. Then the voices of Julian and Dick were heard.

'What's up? Are you girls all right? We're coming!'

The two boys raced over the damp grass in their bare feet, flourishing torches. Julian ran straight into something large, that snorted and whinnied in surprise. Julian yelled. Dick flashed his torch on Julian and started to laugh.

'You ran straight into Dobby,' gasped Dick. 'He must have lumbered all round the caravans making the bumps we heard! It's all right, girls. We can go back to sleep now.'

So back they all went to bed, and this time they slept soundly till the morning.

*Go to **40**.*

George put her hand into the stream to see if she could touch the bottom. The water was very cold, and so clear that she could see every detail of the bed of the stream. The water came halfway up her forearm, and she could see that the caravan's body would be clear of the water when she drove through.

'I don't think we'll have any trouble if we drive through the stream,' she called to Anne. 'I'll go and tell the boys what I'm going to do.'

When George returned she took the reins from Anne.

'Come on!' she said to Trotter, and shook the reins. The big horse ambled forward to the bank of the stream.

Go to **52**.

50

The circus dogs set up a great barking as the red and green caravans drew up. One or two men came out of the tents and looked up the track that led to the camp. They pointed to the children's caravans and seemed astonished.

Ned, with the chimpanzee held firmly by the paw,

came out of the camp in curiosity to see the strange caravans. Julian hailed him.

'Hi, Ned! You didn't think you'd see us here, did you?'

Ned stared at Julian.

If you think Ned seems pleased to see them, go to **57**.
If not, go to **62**.

51

Julian ran back to where Dick was waiting.

'The girls both want to go on to the hills tonight,' he told Dick, 'so let's do that, shall we?' He climbed up on to the seat. 'You drive for a bit, Dick, will you? I want to look at the map.'

Dick shook the reins and Dobby moved forward. The sun was quite low in the sky now, and Dick realised that he was feeling hungry.

'Shall we stop and have some supper, and then go on after we've eaten?' he asked Julian.

'Good idea,' said Julian. 'Look, there's some open ground just ahead. We can pull the caravans off the road and picnic on the grass.'

The two caravans pulled off the road. The horses were tied to the branch of a tree, on the edge of a nearby wood, and before long the four children were enjoying a huge picnic supper.

Go to **55**.

52

Trotter walked steadily forward in to the stream. He splashed through the water and up on to the opposite bank quite happily.

'Well, that wasn't difficult,' said Anne.

George pulled Trotter to a halt so that they could wait for the boys, and she and Anne watched as Julian guided Dobby to the bank, but Dobby stopped dead and refused to go any further! Julian shook the reins.

'Go on, Dobby!' he shouted. 'It's only water! Go on!'

But Dobby wouldn't budge. For some reason he had decided that he was not going to cross the stream, and that was that. All the children shouted at him and tried to encourage him, but without success. George waded back across the stream, got hold of his reins, and tried to make him move by pulling, but Dobby wouldn't move!

Go to **56**.

53

'I think perhaps they've got the horses,' said Anne. 'We'd better go and help them with the harnessing.'

When Julian and Anne reached the other two they found Dobby and Trotter standing quietly cropping the grass, with Dick holding on firmly to their head collars.

'They were just standing behind some trees,' explained George, as the four of them harnessed the horses to the caravans again. 'Have we still got time to get to the hills this evening, Julian?'

Go to **42**.

54

If you have arrived from **58**, *score* ◁ ◁.

'That's Lou, over there,' went on Ned, pointing at a man sitting on the steps of a caravan, reading a newspaper. He was a long-limbed, loose-jointed man with miserable face. The children didn't like the look of him.

'Is he a good acrobat?' asked Anne.

'First class,' answered Ned. 'He can climb anything, anywhere. He could climb that tree over there like a monkey – and I've seen him climb a drainpipe straight up the side of a tall building just like a cat. You should see him on the tightrope, too. He can dance on it!'

Lou felt the children staring at him, and looked up, scowling. Seeing strangers, he got up and loped over to where they were standing.

'Who are these kids?' he asked Ned. 'What are they doing messing about here?'

'We're not messing about,' said Julian politely. 'We came to see Ned. We've met him before.'

Lou looked at Julian as if he was something that smelt nasty.

'Them your caravans?' he asked, jerking his head towards them.

'Yes,' said Julian politely.

'Any grown-ups with you?' asked Lou.

'No,' replied Julian, 'I'm in charge, and we've got a dog that can be very fierce with people he doesn't like!'

Go to **59**.

George finished her piece of cake and yawned.

'If we're going to get to the hills tonight, we'd better get on,' she said. 'I'll go and harness the horses.'

'I'll come with you,' said Dick, scrambling to his feet, and they went towards the tree where Dobby and Trotter had been tied up. There was no sign of them!

'Look, they've broken the branch,' said George. 'Dobby! Trotter!' She waited a moment, then called again. 'Dobby! Trotter!'

By this time Julian and Anne had got up and joined them.

'There's no sign of the horses,' said George. 'I think we'd better split up and look for them. They've probably wandered into the woods. Anne, you go with Julian, and Dick and I will stick together. We'll search this side of the wood, and you two try the other side.'

If you want to go with Julian and Anne, go to **60**.

If you want to go with Dick and George, go to **45**.

56

The four children looked at each other in despair.

'What *are* we going to do?' said Dick. 'Do you think we should go and find a bridge, Julian?'

'It looks as if we'll have to,' replied his brother. 'You are a nuisance, Dobby!'

Just then Anne had an idea. She disappeared into the caravan and came out a moment later with a tube of mints in her hand. She waded across the stream, put a mint into her hand, and held it out to Dobby. Dobby snaffled the mint and looked at Anne as if asking for another one. Anne put another mint on the palm of her hand, and held it just out of Dobby's reach. As he walked towards her to take the mint, she kept backing away from him, and before he knew it, he was through the stream and out the other side! When he was safe on the far bank Anne gave him two more mints, and made a big fuss of him.

'That was very clever of you, Anne,' said Julian. 'I'd forgotten how much old Dobby likes mints!'

Anne and George climbed back on to the front of their caravan, and soon the four of them were in sight of the circus camp.

Go to **46**.

57

Suddenly Ned gave a yell. 'It's you kids I saw a way back on the road. What are *you* doing here? Are those your caravans? They're nice, aren't they?'

'Seeing all your circus caravans going by gave us the idea of borrowing some caravans and coming away for a holiday,' explained Dick. 'We'd love to see round the circus camp and meet all the animals, if you'd show us, Ned.'

' 'Course I will,' said Ned, 'but it would be best to do it when my uncle, Tiger Dan, isn't here. He don't like strangers wandering round the camp.'

'Why is he called Tiger Dan?' asked George curiously.

'Because of his rages,' answered Ned. 'No one in the circus likes him much except Lou, the acrobat – and nobody likes Lou much, either!'

Go to **54**.

58

Ned climbed up beside Julian and Dick. It was rather a squash, but nobody minded that.

'Are these your caravans?' asked Ned. 'They're nice, aren't they?'

'Seeing all your circus vans going by gave us the idea of borrowing some caravans and coming away for a holiday,' explained Julian. 'We wanted to see the circus camp, if we can, and meet some of the animals.'

'I'd be glad to show you around,' said Ned, 'though if my uncle comes back, you'll have to hide.'

'Why is he called Tiger Dan?' asked Dick.

'Because of his terrible rages,' answered Ned, as Julian halted Dobby by the circus camp. 'No one in the circus likes him much except Lou, the acrobat – and no one likes Lou much, either!'

Go to **54**.

59

Timmy clearly didn't like Lou. He stood near him, growling deep in his throat. Lou kicked out at him.

George caught hold of Timmy's collar just in time. 'Down, Timmy down!' she ordered. Then she turned on Lou, her eyes blazing.

'Don't you dare kick my dog!' she shouted. 'Just keep out of his way, do you hear!'

Lou stared at George with contempt.

'You clear out,' he said. 'We don't want no kids messing about here. And I ain't afraid of no dog. We've got ways of dealing with bad dogs.'

'What do you mean by that?' yelled George, still in a furious temper, but Lou didn't answer. He went up the steps of his caravan and slammed the door.

'Now you've done it!' said Ned dismally. 'If Lou catches you around here, he'll turn you out. He's – oh no, that chimp's gone inside one of your caravans!'

Go to **64**.

60

Julian and Anne walked through the wood, calling the two horses from time to time. There was a wire fence at the back of the wood, with a small field on the other side. They walked all the way along the fence, but there was no gate in it, neither was there any gap in the wire.

'Well, they certainly couldn't have got through this wire,' said Julian. 'We'd better go back and find the others. Once we've found the horses we'll have to head for the nearest farm and stay there overnight. We won't have time to get to the hills now.'

Just then they caught sight of Dick outside the wood. He was waving his arms and shouting.

Go to **53**.

61

When darkness fell that night, there were clouds across the sky for the first time. Not a star showed and there was no moon. It was pitch black, and Julian, looking out of the window of his caravan, could not even see a shimmer of water from the lake.

He got into his bunk and pulled the covers up. In the other caravan George and Anne were asleep. Timmy was on George's feet, as usual. Suddenly his ears perked up. He raised his head and growled softly in his throat, and sat there stiffly, listening. Then he growled again, more loudly. George woke up.

'What is it, Timmy?' she whispered. 'Can you hear something?'

George strained her ears, but she couldn't hear anything. Timmy was still sitting up, but he had stopped growling. George lay down again.

If you think George should go back to sleep, go to **66**.
If not, go to **71**.

62

'Don't you remember us, Ned?' asked Julian. 'We spoke to you when the circus passed our house, about a week ago.'

'Never seen you before in my life,' said Ned angrily. 'Now get out of here. My uncle, Tiger Dan, don't like no strangers hanging round the camp.'

Julian stared at Ned in amazement. He was just about to try and explain to Ned who they were, when Ned winked at him. Obviously Ned was trying to tell him something.

'Go on, off with you!' said Ned, and he winked again.

Julian turned Dobby round, followed by George and Trotter, and they left the camp.

Go to **65**.

63

If you have arrived from **74**, *score* ◯⌐.

What were they doing there? Had they come to steal something from the caravans? George wished she could tell Julian and Dick, but she didn't like to go out of her caravan in case the men heard her.

At first she couldn't hear anything they were saying. Then one raised his voice.

'OK. That's settled.' Then came the sound of footsteps again, this time towards George's caravan. The men walked straight into the side of it, exclaimed in surprise and pain, and began to feel about to see what they had walked into.

'It's the caravans belonging to those dratted kids!' exclaimed Lou. 'I told them to clear off!'

He rapped loudly on the walls of the caravan, and Anne woke up with a jump. Timmy barked in rage. Suddenly Julian opened the door of his caravan and flashed his torch on the two men.

'What are you doing round here at this time of night?' he asked angrily. 'Go away and let us get back to sleep!'

Go to **67**.

George's argument with Lou was forgotten as they all rushed to get Pongo out of the caravan. Ned gave the chimp a scolding, and Pongo looked so dejected they all laughed!

'Would you and Pongo like to stay and have tea with us?' Julian asked Ned.

'Oh, yes, please,' said Ned.

They had a very pleasant tea. They all sat out on the heather, on the shady side of the green caravan. Pongo sat beside Anne, taking bits of sandwich from her most politely. Ned made everyone laugh, imitating his uncle, Tiger Dan, and turning cartwheels all round the caravan.

'Well, I suppose I'd better be going,' said Ned, when no one could eat any more. 'Will you be camping here for long?'

'Not exactly *here*,' said Julian. 'We thought of going higher up into the hills. It'll be cooler there. We might camp here just for tonight, though. Perhaps we could see round the circus camp tomorrow morning?'

'Not if Lou's there, you can't,' replied Ned. 'Once he's told people to clear out, he means it. But it will be all right if he isn't there. I'll come and tell you.'

'All right,' said Julian. 'If Lou's there tomorrow morning, we'll go on up to the hills, and you can always signal to us if he's out of the camp, and we can come down any time. Make sure you come and see *us*, too.'

'You bet!' said Ned, and he went off, holding Pongo firmly by the paw.

Go to **61**.

65

'Did you see Ned winking at me?' Julian asked Dick in a low voice as they drove away from the circus camp.

'Yes,' replied Dick, 'and I think he *did* remember us, you know.'

'Well, we'd better head up the hill and look for somewhere to stay,' said Julian. 'It's going to be really disappointing if we can't go to see the circus camp, but at least we'll be able to look at it from a distance.'

They had not gone very far when they heard the sound of running feet behind them.

'Hey! Stop!' called a voice, and Ned came running up to the caravan, out of breath. 'I know who you kids are – I remember seeing you outside your house, but when you arrived just now my uncle was there, and he hates strangers coming to the camp. I had to pretend I didn't want you there, otherwise he'd have been furious with me. You can come back to the camp with me now, if you want. Tiger Dan's gone off somewhere – said he wouldn't be back for a while.'

'I *thought* you were trying to tell me something,' said Julian. 'We'd love to come back and see the camp!'

Go to **58**.

George lay awake for some time, listening for any strange noises outside the caravan, but she couldn't hear anything, and after a while she fell asleep again. Timmy settled back on her feet, but he stayed awake. Something didn't seem quite right to him. He was certain that he had heard something or somebody outside the caravan.

In the other caravan Julian was also awake. He had a vague feeling that he had been woken up by something odd, but he couldn't hear anything. Like Timmy, he lay awake, listening.

Go to **74**.

This was quite the wrong thing to say to Tiger Dan and Lou. They were furious.

'Who do you think you are, telling us to go away?'

shouted Dan angrily. 'You're the ones to clear off!
Do you hear?'

Julian spoke politely but determinedly.

'We're going in the morning, as we planned. If
you're suggesting we should go now, you can think
again. Now please go away and leave us in peace.'

'I'll give you what for, speaking to me like
that!' shouted Lou, and he started to remove
his wide leather belt. George let go her hold on
Timmy's collar.

'Go for them, Timmy!' she said. 'But don't bite, just worry.'

Timmy flung himself at the two men. He got hold of Lou's trouser leg, pulled, and ripped it open from knee to ankle.

'Come on!' shouted Dan. 'The dog's mad! Call him off, you kids, and mind you clear out in the morning!'

The two men went off, and the four children went back to bed, all feeling rather shaken.

Go to **70**.

68

'I wonder what those two wanted to say to us,' said Dick. 'It might have been something important.'

'I don't think they could have anything to say to us that wasn't unpleasant,' replied Julian. 'In all the adventures we've had I don't think we've ever come across a nastier pair. I feel very sorry for Ned, having to live with Dan.'

Dick thought of their home and their parents, and all the fun they had, and realised that they were all very lucky, compared to Ned, even if he did live with the circus, and didn't go to school very regularly!

Go to **78**.

69

Luckily, one of the farms in Julian's book was not far away, and soon they had asked the farmer, whose name was Mr Mackie, if they could camp on his land, and arranged to buy food and milk from his wife. The farmer also told them of a good place to camp.

'It's about half a mile from here,' he said. 'There's a nice sheltered hollow by a clump of birch trees. If you pull your caravans in there you'll be sheltered from the wind, and you'll have a fine view of the lake.'

Mrs Mackie sold them all sorts of delicious things to eat, and gave them a bottle of homemade lemonade as well. Then they set off to find the camping place that Mr Mackie had recommended.

'He said the camping place was just off this track,' said Dick, 'so be on the lookout for a grove of birch trees.'

They had not gone much further when Dick gave a shout.

'Look!' he yelled, pointing to his right. 'There's a clump of trees over there!'

'Yes,' said Julian, 'but there's one over there on the other side of the lane as well. I wonder which one it is?'

If you think they should go to the right, go to **76**.
If you think they should go to the left, go to **81**.

The next morning all four awoke early. Nobody felt inclined to lie in and snooze – all of them were anxious to get off before Lou and Dan appeared. They had breakfast and cleared up.

'You catch the horses, Dick, and get them ready,' said Julian.

'I'll come with you,' said George.

Dobby and Trotter were soon harnessed up, and the four children climbed into the driving seats and started off. They had not gone very far when they heard voices behind them, shouting.

'Stop! You kids, stop! We want to talk to you!'

Dick looked round.

'It's Tiger Dan and Lou! What do you think they want? Shall we stop, Julian?' he said.

If you think they should stop, go to **75**.
If you think they should go on, go to **80**.

71

Timmy growled again. George slipped out of her bunk and went to the half-open door of the caravan.

'Don't make a noise, Timmy,' she whispered.

George looked out of the door. She couldn't see anything, because it was so dark, but she could hear voices, low and muffled. They were not very far away. Then she heard a match struck, and in its light she saw two men lighting their cigarettes from the same match. They were Ned's uncle, Tiger Dan, and Lou the acrobat!

Go to **63**.

72

'Never mind, Ned,' said Julian. 'We'll be waiting for you up in the hills. Bring Pongo to see us some time!'

'Right you are!' said Ned. 'As soon as those two are out of the way you can come down to the camp and I'll show you around. OK?'

'Fine,' said Julian, and drove on.

The road wound steadily upwards, snaking backwards and forwards across the hill. Halfway up, the caravans crossed a stone bridge, under which a very swift stream flowed.

'Look!' exclaimed George. 'The stream seems to start from up there.' She pointed up the hill, and they could all see that the stream flowed out of hole in the hillside.

As they were thirsty, they stopped the caravans and went to have a look at the stream, but the water was not clear enough to drink. However, wandering a little further on they found a real spring that gushed up from underneath a stone, cold and clear, and they drank from that.

'Well, we'd better go and see if we can find a farm,' said Julian.

Go to **69**.

When Julian and Dick reached the trees, Julian pulled Dobby to a halt and Dick got down to have a look round. He walked all the way round the little copse, looking for a good place to park the caravans, but there was nowhere suitable.

By this time George and Anne had joined the boys.

'Is this the place that Mr Mackie recommended, Julian?' asked George. 'It hasn't got much of a view, has it?'

George was right, thought Julian as he looked round. The ground was very uneven, and the land rose steeply on three sides of the thicket, so there was very little to see.

'I'll tell you something else,' said Dick, who had been exploring the area. 'There isn't a stream anywhere near, and I for one don't want to have to walk miles to get water, or to wash. I vote we go back and try the other group of trees.'

Go to **83**.

74

Suddenly Timmy jumped off George's bunk and padded over to the door of the caravan, growling softly. George woke up and jumped out of bed.

'Ssh, Timmy,' she whispered, and opened the door of the caravan a crack. She couldn't see anything outside at all because it was so dark, but she could hear voices, low and muffled. They seemed to come from not very far away. Then she heard a match struck, and in its light she saw two men lighting their cigarettes from the same match. She recognised them at once – they were Ned's uncle, Tiger Dan, and Lou the acrobat!

Go to **63**.

'I suppose we'd better find out what they want,' said Julian.

He pulled Dobby to a halt, and the two men came running up.

'You're going, are you?' said Tiger Dan, with an ugly grin on his face. 'Where are you going?'

'Up to the hills,' replied Julian. 'Not that it's anything to do with you.'

'Why don't you go round the foot of the hills, instead of over the top?' said Lou. 'Silly way to go - up there with the caravans dragging them horses back all the way.'

Julian was just about to say that he didn't intend to go right up to the top of the hills and over to the other side, when he stopped himself. No – just as well not to let these fellows know he meant to camp up there, or they might come and worry them all again.

He clicked to Dobby.

'We're going the way we want to go,' he said curtly,

'and that's up the hill. Now, please get out of the way.'

As Dobby was walking straight at them, the men had to jump to one side.

Go to **78**.

76

The two boys looked from one group of trees to the other. Both seemed to be mostly birch trees, easily recognisable by their pale, silvery bark, and the clumps were roughly the same size, so neither of the boys could decide which way to go!

'I vote we try turning right,' said Dick at last. 'After all, we can always come back if it happens to be the wrong one.'

Julian turned the caravan towards the trees. The ground was very rough and bumpy, and the van lurched and jolted as if it were a ship in a storm! Dick had to hang on to the side to stop himself being thrown off.

'I do hope this is the right place,' gasped Julian. 'I don't want to have to come back across this ground!'

Go to **73**.

77

'Look,' said sharp-eyed Anne, 'there's a little boat pushing out on to the lake from just about where the circus camp is. I wonder if it's Ned? Did you bring any binoculars, Julian?'

'Yes, I did,' her brother replied. 'Hang on a second and I'll find them.'

He went into the green caravan, rummaged through the drawers and came out with the binoculars hanging on a strap round his neck.

'Here we are,' he said, and put them to his eyes. 'Yes – I can see the boat clearly now – and it is Ned in it – and he's got Pongo with him!'

Everyone wanted to look through the binoculars to see Ned and Pongo in the boat.

'You know, we could always get Ned to signal to us from the boat when his uncle is away,' suggested Dick. 'He could wave a sheet or something. Then we would know it was safe to go down and visit the camp.'

'Yes, good idea,' said George.

Go to **82**.

*If you have arrived from **68**, score* ⌒1 *.*

Then they all heard the sound of running feet, and Ned came puffing up to the caravan.

'Hey! Where are you all going so early?' he asked. 'Can I come part of the way with you?'

'No you don't,' said his uncle, who had come up behind him. 'I've told these kids to clear out, and they're going. I won't have meddling strangers round the camp, do you hear?'

Ned turned on his heel and started to walk back towards the camp. His hands were jammed in his pockets, and he shuffled along, his head down. The caravans overtook him on the way.

*Go to **72**.*

If you have arrived from **84**, *score* ⌒⊲ .

There was one steep place that forced the children to stay on the track. They went along it to where the track turned a sharp corner round a cliff-like bend – and to their surprise and dismay they walked straight into Tiger Dan and Lou!

'Take no notice,' said Julian in a low voice. 'Keep together and walk straight on. Pretend that Timmy is somewhere behind us.'

'Timmy!' called George at once.

Lou and Dan seemed just as surprised to see them. The two men stopped and looked hard at them, but Julian hurried the others along.

'Hey, wait a minute!' called Dan. 'I thought you had gone off – over the hill top!'

'Sorry, we can't stop!' called back Julian. 'We're in a hurry!'

Lou shouted to the children, trying to make himself sound good-tempered.

'Where are your caravans? Are you camping up here anywhere?'

But the children walked on, and the men had to hurry after them to make them hear.

Go to **86**.

80

'No,' said Julian. 'I don't want to see those two again if we can help it. There's something about them that I really don't like.'

'Hey, you kids! STOP!' yelled Lou again.

Julian shook the reins to make Dobby move faster, but Tiger Dan and Lou came panting up beside the caravan. Julian didn't stop, so the two men had to run alongside, getting more and more out of breath!

'We want to know where you're going to camp,' said Dan. 'We thought we might be able to suggest a good place. We know all this part of the world – we could help you kids.'

Julian shook his head. 'We don't need your help, thank you,' he said.

'You don't know what we could tell you,' shouted Lou. 'You should listen to us.'

But Julian just went on driving, and Tiger Dan and Lou dropped back, muttering angrily to each other.

Go to **68**.

81

Julian hesitated, looking from one clump of trees to the other.

'Let's try the one on the left,' he said finally. 'After all, we can easily come back and try the other one if we're wrong.'

The two caravans trundled down the track to the coppice of trees.

'This has got to be it!' exclaimed Dick. 'Look at the view of the lake we can get from here! It's a fantastic place to camp!'

It certainly was. They could see right down the steep hillside to the lake. Heather grew like a springy purple carpet all over the ground, and red fireweed grew in the crevices to the hill behind. There was even a spring nearby, with cold, clear water.

'Aren't we lucky?' exclaimed Julian with pleasure. 'This is a brilliant place to camp, and nobody will disturb us here!'

Go to **85**.

82

It was a terribly hot day, too hot to do anything – even walk down to the lake and swim. They were all glad they were up the hills, for at least there was a little breeze from time to time.

At tea time they decided they would go down and have a swim about half past six. It would be cooler by then.

They were just about to set off when Julian had a thought.

'George, do you think we should leave Timmy here on guard, in case Tiger Dan and Lou show up?' he asked.

'Oh, poor Timmy, can't he come too?' protested Anne. 'He must be just as hot as we are, and he does enjoy swimming. Let's take him with us, George!'

George hesitated.

If you think that Timmy should be left on guard, go to **87**.
If you think they should take him with them, go to **93**.

83

None of them liked the idea of having to drive the caravans across the bumpy ground again, but there was no way round it, and soon they were back on the lane.

Fortunately there was quite a well-worn track to the other clump of trees, and the two caravans trundled along easily.

'This has to be it!' exclaimed Dick. 'Look at the view of the lake we can get from here! It's a fantastic place to camp!'

It certainly was. They could see right down the steep hillside to the lake. Heather grew like a springy purple carpet all over the ground, and red fireweed grew in the crevices of the hill behind. There was even a spring nearby, with cool, clear water.

'Aren't we lucky?' exclaimed Julian with pleasure. 'This is a brilliant place to stop, and nobody will disturb us here!'

Go to **85**.

The four of them hadn't gone very far when George suddenly stopped.

'Come on, George,' said Dick, 'Why are you standing there like a statue?'

'I've just had a thought about Timmy,' replied George. 'If he goes swimming now, he won't have time to dry off before we go to bed.'

'Does that matter?' said Dick.

'Yes, of course it does,' answered George. 'You know Timmy always sleeps on my bunk, but if he's still soaking wet he'll make the bedclothes all wet too!'

'It's a warm evening,' said Anne. 'Surely he'll be dry before we go to bed?'

George shook her head.

'His coat is so thick that it takes ages to dry, even in hot weather,' she said, 'and I didn't think to bring one of his towels. He really can't have ours! I'll have to send him back to the caravans. Go on, Timmy! Go back and guard the caravans. On guard, Timmy.'

Timmy hesitated for a moment, then trotted obediently back up the hill, while the children went on down to the lake, taking short cuts where they could.

Go to **79**.

85

If you have arrived from **83**, *score* ◠ ◠.

It really was fun settling into that cosy hollow. The two caravans were backed in side by side. The horses were taken to a field where Mr Mackie kept his horses, and turned loose. It was a large field, and had a stone water trough in one corner, so the children knew that Dobby and Trotter would have enough to drink, and plenty of grass to graze on.

At the front of the hollow there was a rocky ledge, flat enough to take plates and cups without spilling anything, and with a tremendous view over the lake.

The children could see faint spirals of smoke coming up from the circus camp far below them.

Go to **77**.

86

'Hey! What's the matter? We only want to know if you're camping here. It's better down below, you know.'

'Keep on walking,' muttered Julian. 'Don't tell them anything. Why do they tell us it's better to camp down below when they were so anxious for us to clear out yesterday. They're mad!'

'Timmy! Timmy!' called George again, hoping that the men would stop following them if they thought Timmy was around.

It did stop them. They gave up going after the children, and didn't shout any more. They turned angrily and went on up the track.

The four children carried on down the hill, and

were soon splashing happily in the icy cold water
of the lake.

Go to **90**.

87

'I really do think we ought to leave Timmy here,'
insisted Julian. 'After all, we don't want Tiger Dan
and Lou sneaking round the caravans, do we?'

'I think you've got a point, Julian,' said George.
She turned to Timmy. 'You're to be on guard,
Timmy,' she said firmly. 'Don't let anyone come
near our caravans. On guard, Timmy!'

'Woof!' said Timmy dismally, and put his tail
down, but he trotted off obediently to lie down
in the shade.

The children set off down the hill with their
swimming things, taking short cuts where they could.

Go to **79**.

They all listened hard.

'I don't think we'd be able to hear Timmy barking,' said Dick. 'We're too far from the caravans for that, aren't we?'

'Oh, no,' said Julian positively. 'On a warm still day like this sound carries a long way. Still, I don't think that was Timmy. It didn't sound deep enough for his bark. Are there any big dogs with the circus, Ned?'

Ned shook his head. 'All the circus dogs are small,' he answered. 'Small dogs are better at doing tricks than large ones.'

'I remember you had a couple of performing dogs with you when we first met you – when the circus went past our house,' said Anne. 'What were those two dogs called, Ned?'

'Barker and Growler,' answered Ned, 'and I think that's Growler you can hear now. His bark is quite deep for a small dog.'

Go to **96**.

89

Lou began to lose his temper. 'Well, are you going to move or ain't you?' he said. 'We've told you we want this bit of the hill. You can come down and camp by the lake again if you want to.'

'Yes – you come,' said Tiger Dan, to the children's growing astonishment. 'You can bathe in the lake every day then, and Ned here can show you round the camp.'

It was Ned's turn to be amazed.

'Didn't you tell me not to have nothing to do with these kids?' he demanded. 'What's your game? You've never had animals up in the hills before!'

'Shut up!' said Dan, so fiercely that all the children were shocked. Lou nudged Dan, and he made an effort to look pleasant again.

'We saw how well Ned was getting on with you, and we didn't want to spoil your fun,' he began again. 'You come on down and camp by the lake, and Ned'll show you everything in the circus. Can't say fairer than that.'

Julian shook his head firmly.

'We've decided to stay here, thank you,' he said, and he turned on his heel and walked towards the caravans, followed by the others.

Go to **95**.

90

Suddenly Ned appeared on the bank, waving and yelling.

'I'm coming in too. Lou and my uncle have gone off somewhere!'

'We met them just now as we were coming down the hill,' said George. 'They were going up into the hills.'

'Going up into the hills?' said Ned, astonished. 'Whatever for? They don't go and fetch things from the farm – they leave that to the others.'

'Well, we met them,' said Dick. 'They seemed very surprised to see us.'

Ned joined the others in the water. 'I've had a bad day,' he said. 'Tiger Dan was real furious with me for making friends with you. He says I'm not to go talking to no strangers no more. I'll just have to be careful he never sees me with you, that's all.'

'We saw you out in your boat with Pongo,' said Julian. 'We thought if ever you wanted to signal to us you could go out in your boat and wave a handkerchief or something. I've got some binoculars, so we can easily see you. Then we would know that the coast was clear, and we could come down.'

Go to **94**.

Before long Ned was back, accompanied by the two rough-haired terriers the children had seen at their first meeting with him. Barker and Growler jumped straight into the lake and had a wonderful time, swimming and playing about. They obviously enjoyed cooling down after the hot day. The children got back in the water and had another swim. Barker made Anne laugh by chasing after her as she swam and trying to lick her feet!

'Oh, Ned, they're brilliant dogs!' exclaimed Dick.

'Yes,' replied Ned. 'I'm real fond of them – sometimes they're all that keeps me going when Tiger Dan's giving me a hard time.'

The four of them gazed at Ned sympathetically. Imagine having to depend on two dogs for affection!

Ned grinned at them.

'Don't look like that,' he said. 'I don't have such a bad life, you know!'

When they had all finished their swim, Ned shooed Barker and Growler back to the camp.

Then they all started back up the hill to the caravans. Suddenly a dog began to bark.

Go to **99**.

The next morning Dick went to the farm to buy some more supplies from Mrs Mackie. She was delighted to see him, and gave him two large baskets full of delicious food.

'Slices of ham I've cured myself,' she said, lifting up the white cloth that covered one of the baskets. 'There are some lettuces and radishes that I pulled myself this morning, and some more tomatoes. In the other basket there are milk, eggs, bread, butter and a tin of shortbread that I made myself. There's a bone for the dog, too.'

'Gosh, thanks a lot, Mrs Mackie!' said Dick in delight. He paid for the food and set off back to the caravans.

When he arrived, Julian called to him: 'Ned's out in his boat. Come and look. He's waving something that looks like a tablecloth. It's obviously all right for us to go down to the camp.'

'Shall we take a picnic lunch down with us?' said Dick. 'I think it would be a good idea!'

'You and your stomach!' laughed Anne. 'I'll go and get something ready. Come and give me a hand, will you, George?'

In no time at all Anne and George had prepared a big picnic, including enough food for Ned as well. Then they collected their swimming things. Julian decided that they would have to leave Timmy behind to guard the caravans, since Tiger Dan and Lou had been snooping around the day before. Timmy was not pleased to be left behind, but he settled down obediently in the shade as the children set off down the hill.

It didn't take them long to get down to the camp, and Ned, Pongo, Barker and Growler were waiting for them.

Go to **97**.

93

Timmy saw them all looking at him, so he wagged his tail, putting his head on one side and gazing at George so pleadingly that she laughed.

'Timmy knows we're off somewhere, and he doesn't want to be left behind! Let's take him with us, Julian!'

'All right,' agreed Julian, a bit reluctantly. He was not very happy about leaving the caravans unguarded with two nasty characters like Lou and Dan around, but there was no reason to suppose they would leave the circus camp at that time of day – they would be busy with their evening meal.

'Come on, then, Timmy!' said George, and the four children and Timmy set off down the hill.

Go to **84**.

'Right,' said Ned. 'I'll do as you say.'

When they had finished their swim, Julian asked Ned if he would like to go back and have supper with them. Ned hesitated. He very much wanted to, but he was afraid of meeting Lou and his uncle coming back from their walk.

'We can easily look out for them,' said Dick, 'and if we see or hear them you can hide behind a bush.'

'Then I'll come,' said Ned. 'By the way, where's Timmy?'

'We left him on guard,' answered Dick. 'We were afraid those two chaps would go poking round our caravans.'

Dick suddenly remembered that he had been talking about Ned's uncle, and went red. Ned wasn't offended, however.

'Dan's not *really* my uncle,' he said cheerfully. 'My mother and father left a bit of money for me when they died, so Dan took me in. It was the money he wanted, though, not me. Soon as I'm old enough I'm going to clear off and join another circus. I want to work with horses, but the chap in charge of ours won't let me near them. He's jealous because I can handle them so well.'

'Listen!' said Anne suddenly. In the distance a dog was barking.

'Probably one of the circus dogs,' said Ned.

Julian stood still, listening. 'It could be Timmy,' he said.

If you think it's a circus dog, go to **88**.
If you think it's Timmy, go to **99**.

95

Ned was extremely puzzled by what Dan and Lou had said, but he shrugged his shoulders and made up his mind to enjoy having supper with the others.

Anne boiled eggs until they were hard, and cut sandwiches which she filled with potted meat and tomatoes. She got out the lemonade that Mrs Mackie had given them, too. They had a fantastic supper, sitting on the flat rock that overlooked the lake.

Eventually Ned got up regretfully.

'I'll have to go,' he said. 'I've still got a few jobs to do, but if you'd like to come down and see the animals tomorrow, I'll signal to show that the coast is clear – I expect you'd rather not bump into Tiger Dan and Lou again. Well – bye for now. Thanks for the supper.'

Go to **92**.

96

'I'd love to see Barker and Growler again,' said Anne. 'Could you go and get them, Ned?'

Ned hesitated.

'Oh, I don't see why not,' he said. 'I usually take Barker and Growler for a walk in the evening, when it's cooler. You wait here, and I'll go and get them.'

'Thanks, Ned!' exclaimed Anne. She was longing to see the two clever dogs again. Ned went off to the circus camp to get them, and the others lay back on their towels, drying off after their swim.

Go to **91**.

97

Ned was grinning from ear to ear.

'You saw my signal all right?' he asked. 'Tiger Dan seems to have taken to you – says I'm to show you round and let you see anything you want.'

'Where shall we put the swimming things and our food?' asked Anne. 'It ought to be somewhere cool.'

'Put them in my caravan,' said Ned, and led them to a caravan painted blue and yellow, with red wheels. Julian was looking thoughtful, and as Ned went to open the caravan door, Julian turned to the others.

'You know, I really do think it's a bit suspicious, Tiger Dan telling Ned we're welcome here,' he said. 'I wonder if we should go back to the caravans and make sure they're safe. I think Tiger Dan and Lou want us out of the way, for some reason. Come on, we can see round the camp later on.'

'Oh, no!' said George. 'I'm sure everything will be all right. Let's stay here!'

If you think they should go back to the caravans, go to **102**.
If you think they should stay at the circus camp, go to **107**.

98

They had their meal sitting by the lake. It glittered at their feet, calm and blue, and looked very inviting. They were all sleepy after lunch, so they had a short nap, then decided to go and see the monkeys. When they got back to the camp they found it alive with people, all excited and yelling.

'What's up?' asked Ned. 'Jumping Jimmy, the monkeys are loose!'

So they were. Wherever they looked, the children saw a small brown monkey, chattering to itself, on the roof of a caravan or tent.

'Lucilla will be able to get them back,' said Ned. 'Hi, look – there she is! Now we'll be all right.'

A little wizened old woman was hurrying towards the camp. She looked a bit like a monkey herself, Anne thought. Her eyes were bright and sharp, and her tiny hands clutched a red shawl round her.

'Your monkeys are out! LUCILLA! Your monkeys are out!' yelled the camp children.

Lucilla stood still and held out her arms. She spoke some words in a language the children didn't understand, and one by one the wandering monkeys came scampering over to her, making little chattering sounds of love and welcome.

Go to **100**.

*If you have arrived from **91**, score* ⌀ ⌀ ⌀.

'It's Timmy,' said George positively. 'I'd know that bark anywhere!'

As they came up to the clump of trees, they could see why Timmy had been barking. Lying down on the grass in the shade were Lou and Tiger Dan!

It was too late for Ned to hide. The men saw him at once, and they got up and came towards the children. Julian looked at them. To his surprise, they both looked quite amiable. A faint scowl came over Tiger Dan's face when he saw Ned, but it passed at once.

'We see you're camping up here,' said Lou, with a false smile. 'Aren't you going over the hill?'

'I don't think that's any concern of yours,' said Julian mildly. 'You told us to clear out from down below, and we did. What we do now is nothing to do with you.'

'Oh yes, it is,' said Tiger Dan, sounding as if he

was being pleasant with great difficulty. 'We come up here to plan a place for some of our animals, and we don't want you to be in no danger, see?'

'We won't be in any danger,' said Julian. 'We have Timmy with us – and if we want help, the farmer and his men are near by.'

Go to **89**.

After tea the children wandered round the camp looking at the wagons. No one took much notice of them – the circus people had accepted them as Ned's friends.

There were a lot of big wagons, which contained all the equipment for the Big Top. Then they came to a small wagon covered with a tightly-fitting tarpaulin.

'What's in this wagon?' asked Anne.

'Don't know,' replied Ned. 'That cart belongs to Tiger Dan. He won't never let me unpack it. I don't know what he keeps in there. I thought I'd have a peep one day, but Dan caught me and he was real angry at me. Funny thing is, sometimes that cart is crammed full, and sometimes it isn't. Maybe Lou puts some of his things there too.'

'Well, nobody could get anything in there at the moment!' exclaimed Julian. 'It's full to bursting.'

'Let's have a quick look under the tarpaulin,' said Dick. 'There's nobody around.'

'Oh, no,' said Anne. 'I don't think we should do that.'

If you think they should look under the tarpaulin, go to **105.**

If you think they should not, go to **111.**

101

If you have arrived from **106**, *score* ♈.

'Where have you been?' asked Anne.

'Timmy fell over a ledge of rock,' replied Dick. 'It took us quite a long time to rescue him!'

'What on earth was he doing to make him fall like that?' said Julian.

'I expect he was chasing rabbits!' said George, and by the way Timmy looked at her, she knew she was right!

Leaving Timmy on guard, the four of them made

their way back down the hill to where Ned was waiting.

'Finally!' he said. 'You kids have been a long time. Dan and Lou came back while you were gone – asked if you'd been snooping around. I told him you hadn't. After all, you weren't *snooping*, were you?'

'Are Dan and Lou still here?' asked Julian.

'No,' said Ned. 'They've gone off again – goodness knows where. Come on, I'll show you the camp.'

Go to **107**.

102

Anne's face fell. 'I want to stay here and see the animals, Julian!' she said. 'What makes you think we should go back to the caravans?'

'It's just a feeling I've got,' answered Julian. 'I think we should go and see that everything is all right. What about you, Ned? Are you going to stay here, or would you like to come with us?'

Ned shook his head.

'I'd like to come with you,' he said, 'but I think I'd better stay here and finish one or two odd jobs that Dan told me to do. You kids will come back, won't you?'

'Oh yes,' said Dick. 'We won't be long.'

The four children toiled back up the hill. It was another blazing hot day, and they all thought longingly about a swim in the icy water of the lake but they would have to wait!

'I can't hear Timmy barking,' said Dick, 'so there can't be anyone hanging round the caravans. What do you think might have happened, Julian? Do you think Dan and Lou might be snooping around?'

'I'm afraid of something like that,' admitted Julian.

When they came in sight of the two caravans, everything looked peaceful. There was no sign of anyone, or of any disturbance. As they got closer however, they realised that something was very wrong indeed. There was no sign of Timmy!

George went as white as a sheet. She rushed forward shouting at the top of her voice.

'Timmy! TIMMY!'

But no big black and white dog came bounding to meet her.

She turned anxiously to the others.

'What do you suppose has happened to him?' she whispered. 'Do you think those awful men might have come and taken him away?'

'No, of course not,' said Julian reassuringly 'Timmy would never let anyone take him away – think how fierce he can be! I'm sure he can't be far away. We'd better split up and look for him. Anne, you come with me, and Dick, you go with George.'

They set off in different directions, calling Timmy's name.

If you want to go with Julian and Anne, go to **110**.
If you want to go with Dick and George, go to **115**.

''Course not!' replied Ned. 'Old Lady wouldn't hurt anyone, would you, big one?'

A small man came up. He had bright eyes which shone as if they had been polished, and a very wide grin.

'Good morning,' he said. 'How do you like my Old Lady? Like to see her play cricket?'

'Oh *yes!*' said everyone, and the small man produced a cricket bat and held it out to Old Lady. She took it in her trunk and waved it about. Ned slipped deftly off her head.

'I'll play with her, Larry,' he said, and took the ball from the small man. He threw it to Old Lady and she hit it smartly with the bat. It sailed over their heads. Julian fetched the ball and threw it at the elephant, and again the great creature hit the ball with a bang. Soon all the children were playing with Old Lady and enjoying it very much.

When they had finished their game Ned fetched Pongo, the chimpanzee, who was delighted to see them all. Then they went to see the dogs and let them out. Barker and Growler followed the children round the camp. Their next stop was to see the beautiful circus horses with their satiny coats. They were being exercised in a field by a tall, slim young fellow called Rossy. Ned delighted the others by riding one of the horses standing up! The morning passed very quickly, seeing all the animals, and soon it was time for lunch.

Go to **98.**

104

They all looked at Barker, who was gnawing some meat on the ground. Growler ran to it too, but Timmy wouldn't go near it. He put his tail down, and Pongo hid his furry face behind his paws.

'Funny,' said one of the children, puzzled by the strange behaviour of the animals. Then suddenly they understood – for poor Barker gave a terrible whine, shivered from head to foot, then rolled over on his side.

Ned ran forward and kicked Growler away from the meat.

'Jimmy!' he yelled. 'The meat must be poisoned!'

He picked Barker up, and to their dismay the children saw that he was crying.

'I got to take him to Lucilla,' said Ned. 'She's a wonder with sick animals.'

'Do you want one of us to come with you, Ned?' asked Julian.

Ned hesitated.

If you think Ned goes back on his own, go to **109.**
If you think one of them goes with him, go to **116.**

105

Ned looked worried.

'I don't think we should,' he said. 'Supposing

Dan or Lou came back and caught us? They'd be furious.'

'One of us could be a look-out,' suggested George, who was as eager to see into the mysterious wagon as Dick. 'Anne, you wouldn't mind being our look-out, would you?'

Anne hesitated. She didn't like the idea of suddenly finding Dan or Lou arriving in a rage, but on the other hand she didn't really want to look under the tarpaulin. She nodded.

'I don't mind being a look-out,' she said, 'but don't be too long, will you?'

Dick laughed.

'I'm sure you think we're going to find a body under there, Anne!' he said.

Anne shuddered. 'What a horrible thought, Dick! You are a beast.'

Go to **112**.

'What's the matter?' called Julian.

'I've caught my foot in a bramble,' Anne replied. 'I seem to be stuck.'

'Oh, *Anne!*' said Julian in exasperation. 'Now we'll *never* catch Timmy!'

At that moment they heard a movement among the leaves nearby, and a small head with two huge brown eyes appeared.

'Look, Julian!' whispered Anne. 'It's a deer!'

Suddenly the little creature bounded off into the wood.

'So, it wasn't Timmy after all,' said Julian, unhooking the bramble from Anne's jeans. 'Come on, let's get back to the others.'

They made their way back to the caravans, to find George, Dick and Timmy waiting for them.

Go to **101.**

If you have arrived from **101**, *score* ⋈ ⋈ ⋈ ⋈ ⋈.

Julian still felt uneasy, but he shrugged his shoulders and grinned.

'OK,' he said. 'Let's look round, shall we?'

'What would you like to see first?' asked Ned. 'The elephant? Come on then.'

They went to the tree to which Old Lady, the elephant, was tied. She curled her trunk round Ned and looked at the children with small, intelligent eyes.

'Well, Old Lady,' said Ned. 'Want a bath?'

The elephant trumpeted and made the children jump.

'I'll take you later on,' promised Ned. 'Now – hup, hup, hup!'

At these words the elephant curled her trunk tightly round Ned's waist and lifted him bodily into the air, placing him gently on her big head!

Anne gasped.

'Oh! Did she hurt you, Ned?'

Go to **103**.

108

'I think it would be best if you came and pulled with me,' shouted Dick.

'OK!' called George, and soon her head appeared over the edge. Scrambling to her feet, she took one of the reins from Dick, and together they began to pull. It was easy with two of them, but after a few seconds, Timmy began to whimper.

'It's no good,' said George. 'Without me holding him from underneath, he's being scraped against the side. I'll have to go down again. See if you can find a tree to wind the reins around.'

Go to **113**.

'No thanks,' said Ned. 'Dan or Lou might be back, and it's best if they don't see you with me.'

Carrying Barker in his arms, with Pongo and Growler behind him, Ned stumbled down the hill. The others looked at each other in dismay. What a dreadful thing to have happened!

George was as white as a sheet, and she kept Timmy close by her.

'Who on earth would be unkind enough to feed a dog poisoned meat?' asked Anne in bewilderment.

'Who do you think?' said George fiercely.

Go to **121**.

110

'Which way shall we go, Julian?' asked Anne.

'I think we'd better go towards the farm,' replied her brother. 'I suppose it's possible that Mr

Mackie or his wife might have seen Timmy, or perhaps one of the farm workers may be able to tell us something. Don't look so worried, Anne! Timmy can look after himself.'

They walked down the track leading to the farm, still calling Timmy's name at intervals. Suddenly Anne stood still.

'Come on, Anne,' said Julian impatiently. 'What are you standing there like a statue for?'

'I thought I heard a dog barking,' said Anne. 'Ssh!'

They both strained their ears, and this time Julian heard barking too.

Go to **114.**

111

'We'd better not,' said Ned. 'Some of the other circus folk might see us and tell Dan, and he'd be furious.'

They lost interest in the wagon and wandered

round looking at the circus props. There were gilt chairs and tables, the shining poles used for the tightrope, gaily painted stools for the performing dogs to sit on, and all sorts of other things.

'Look at the time,' said Julian at last, 'don't you think it's time we were getting back for supper? It's seven o'clock, and I'm starving. Why don't you come up with us for supper, Ned?'

'Oh, yes, I'd like that,' said Ned. 'I'll bring Barker and Growler, too, and Pongo, if you don't mind.'

Go to **117**.

112

Anne walked away to a place where she could see the main track that led to the camp, and the others turned back to the mysterious wagon. The tarpaulin was tied down tightly with strong ropes, and Julian could see that it would take a long time to undo them.

'I think we'd better try and pull one of the corners up,' he said. 'Then we can have a quick look underneath.'

They all set to work, trying to pull the taut tarpaulin off the wagon, and eventually one corner was loose. Dick held it up, and Julian looked underneath.

Go to **119**.

113

If you have arrived from **108**, *score* ◯ᕁ.

Dick looked round. Not very far away was a gnarled, sturdy-looking ash tree. If he wound the reins round that, it would take some of the strain and make it easier for him to pull Timmy up. The reins were very long, and would easily reach the tree.

'Hold on a minute,' he called down to George, 'I'm going to try winding the reins round a tree. I'll give a shout when I'm ready for you to lift Timmy.'

Dick walked over to the tree and hitched the reins around it.

'George!' he shouted. 'Lift Timmy!'

Dick leant back and pulled as hard as he would have done in a tug of war. It was hard work, but eventually Timmy's head appeared at the top of the ledge, and he scrabbled up over the edge.

George climbed up after Timmy, untied the reins and quickly checked him over to see that he hadn't hurt himself. Then she and Dick took him back to the caravans, where Julian and Anne were waiting.

Go to **101**.

114

'Timmy! Timmy!' called Julian, and was answered by more barking. 'That sounds like Timmy. Come on, Anne!'

The two of them ran off the track, across a field,

then scrambled breathlessly over a gate leading into a small wood.

As Anne jumped to the ground her keen eyes caught a movement amongst the trees.

Go to **118**.

115

Dick and George decided to look round the caravans first. There was no sign of Timmy anywhere. They had moved quite a long way from the caravans when Dick heard a noise he couldn't place. He stood still and listened, and the noise came again. It was a dog, whimpering!

'George!' he yelled. 'George, come here!'

George came running up, out of breath.

'Have you found him?' she panted.

'I think so,' said Dick. 'I hear a dog whimpering – I think it's coming from further down the hill.'

George and Dick were standing on a shelf of

rock like the one they used for meals. They both ran to the edge and looked over. About four metres below them, on a tiny ledge of rock, sat Timmy!

'Oh, Timmy!' said George, as he looked up at her, 'thank goodness you're safe!'

'Yes,' said Dick, 'but how are we going to get him off that ledge of rock?'

Go to **120**.

116

Barker gave a whimper, and wriggled restlessly. Ned looked down at him.

'Poor old Barker!' he said. 'Poor old thing Lucilla will put you right.' He looked up at the others. 'I would like one of you to come down to the camp with me – just till I've got Barker settled with Lucilla.'

'Yes, of course,' said Julian. 'I'll come with you, Ned.'

Ned and Julian hurried off down the hill to the circus camp, with Barker whining feebly in Ned's arms, and the others sat down to wait. Anne suggested getting supper, but nobody felt very hungry, so they decided to wait until Julian came back.

George was as white as a sheet, and she kept Timmy close by her.

'Who on earth would be unkind enough to feed a dog poisoned meat?' Anne wondered.

'Who do you think?' answered George.

Go to **124.**

117

If you have arrived from **119***, score* ⌣ ⌣.

They set off up the hill, tired with their long and exciting day. Anne began to plan what they would have for supper. She thought ham and tomatoes

and new bread would be nice.

They all heard Timmy barking excitedly as they approached the caravans. He barked without stopping, loudly and determinedly.

'He sounds cross,' said Dick. 'Poor old Timmy! He must think we've deserted him.'

As soon as he saw George, Timmy flung himself on her as if he hadn't seen her for a year. Barker and Growler were pleased to see him too, and as for Pongo, he was delighted. He shook hands with Timmy's tail several times, and looked disappointed that Timmy took no notice of him.

'Hallo! What's Barker gnawing at?' said Dick suddenly. 'Raw meat! How do you suppose that got here? Do you suppose the farmer came by and gave Timmy some? Why hasn't he eaten it, then?'

Go to **104**.

118

'Julian, quick, look!' gasped Anne, pointing into the wood.

Julian caught sight of a moving shape disappearing into the trees.

They crashed through the undergrowth in hot pursuit.

Suddenly, Anne gave a cry and fell over.

Go to **106**.

'I can't see a thing,' he said. 'Has anyone got a torch?'

'I've got one in the caravan,' said Ned, and he ran off to get it. He came back a minute later carrying a small torch that gave only a feeble light.

'It's not very good,' he said to Julian, 'but it might help a bit.'

Julian plunged back under the tarpaulin and flashed the torch around. All he could make out were cardboard boxes – the sort that supermarkets used – with newspapers stuck over the top. He couldn't look inside any of the boxes without pulling the newspaper off, and he didn't want to do that, because Dan and Lou would know that someone had been touching them. He wriggled out and stood up.

'There's nothing exciting in there,' he said, 'just some cardboard boxes, all covered with newspaper. Come on, let's put the tarpaulin back.'

They pulled the tarpaulin back into place, and Dick looked at his watch.

'Seven o'clock!' he exclaimed. 'Come on, let's go back and have some supper. Ned, would you like to come with us?'

'Oh, yes,' said Ned. 'I'll bring Barker and Growler, and Pongo, if that's all right.'

Go to **117**.

120

'What we need is a rope,' said George. 'Then I could climb down to Timmy, tie the rope round him, and you could haul him up. Did we bring a rope with us?'

'No,' said Dick, 'I don't think we did. We haven't even got sheets we could tie together – we all brought sleeping bags.'

'I know!' said George triumphantly. 'Trotter's harness! If we unbuckle the reins, we could use those. They're long and very strong.'

'Good idea!' exclaimed Dick. 'I'll go back to

the caravan and fetch them – you stay here and comfort Timmy.'

He ran off towards the caravans, and George lay down on her stomach with her head sticking over the edge of the rock, and talked to Timmy. Fortunately he was being very sensible, sitting quietly on the little shelf of rock, and listening to George's soothing words.

It wasn't long before Dick came back carrying the reins.

'I'll climb down to Timmy, then you lower the reins down to me,' instructed George as she swung herself over the edge and inched her way down the side of the hill. Timmy continued to sit very still. Once George had reached the ledge, she called up to Dick.

'Right, Dick, throw the reins down!'

Dick lay flat on his stomach on the edge of the hill and lowered one of the reins to George. She fastened it round Timmy's body, just behind his front legs. Being leather, the reins were difficult to knot, but at last she managed a knot that felt firm when she pulled on it. Dick lowered the other reins, and George knotted it round Timmy just in front of his back legs.

'When I shout, you lift Timmy up, and I'll pull,' called Dick. 'Ready?'

'Ready!' answered George.

Dick wriggled back from the edge, holding the ends of the two reins, and got to his feet.

'Right, George,' he shouted. 'Lift Timmy up!' At the same time Dick began to pull. It was hard work, because Timmy was a big, heavy dog. Dick pulled and pulled, but it was no good. He couldn't lift Timmy more than a few inches. Eventually he stopped.

'George!' he shouted. 'I can't manage this! Can you climb up and help me?'

'Why don't you wind the reins round a tree or something,' George called back.

If you think George should climb up and help, go to **108**.
If you think Dick should attach the reins to something, go to **113**.

*If you have arrived from **124**, score* ⌒⌐ .

'We can't leave Timmy here on his own again,' said George. 'Anything might happen.'

'What is it about this place that makes Dan and Lou so anxious to get us away from here?' wondered Julian. 'They're dodgy, those two.'

Nobody felt very much like eating that evening. Anne got out some bread and butter and jam, and they each had a slice, but that was all. It had been a terrible end to a lovely day.

They all went to bed early, and nobody objected when Julian said he was going to lock both the caravans.

'Not that I think either Dan or Lou will be up here tonight,' he said, 'but you never know!'

Whether anyone came or not the children didn't know, for although Timmy began to bark frantically in the middle of the night, there was nothing to be seen when Julian opened his door and switched on his torch.

Go to **127**.

122

When Julian came near their camping place, Dick called to him excitedly.

'Hey, Julian! Come and look through the binoculars. Ned's out in his boat with Pongo, and I can't make out what it is they're both waving.'

Julian took the binoculars and looked through them. Far down the hill, on the surface of the lake, floated Ned's little boat. In it was Ned, and with him was Pongo. Both of them were waving something bright red.

'Can't see what they're waving – but that doesn't matter,' said Julian. 'The thing is, what they're waving is red, not white, and red is for danger.'

'You're right! I didn't think of that,' said Dick. 'I wonder what's up?'

'Well, it's clear we'd better not go down to the camp today,' said Julian. 'It's also clear that whatever danger there is must be pretty bad, because both Ned *and* Pongo are waving red cloths. *Double* danger!'

Go to **129**.

123

They searched carefully, looking into hollows and rabbit holes, and in clumps of trees. Anne thought it would have been much easier if she had known what she was looking for, but she didn't say anything! The ground around the caravans was bumpy, and covered with heather. There were small clumps of trees here and there, occasional rocky outcrops that looked as if they might have caves concealed in them, but neither Julian nor Anne could find anything.

'Come on,' said Julian at last. 'I don't think there's

much point in spending any more time looking – it's nearly ten o'clock. We'd better go back and find the others.'

They walked back to the caravans, but only Dick was there.

'Where's George?' asked Anne.

Go to **126**.

124

Julian and Ned made their way down the hill as fast as they could, with Growler racing after them. When they got to the camp Ned shouted for Lucilla.

'Lucilla! LUCILLA! Barker's sick! I think he's eaten some poison.'

The tiny, monkey-like woman came out of her caravan and took the sick dog out of Ned's arms.

'Don't you worry, Ned,' she said. 'Old Lucilla

knows what to do for a sick animal. Just you leave him with me.'

Lucilla disappeared into her caravan carrying Barker, and Julian looked at Ned.

'Will you be all right now, Ned?' He asked.

Ned nodded, making an attempt to smile, but not succeeding.

'Barker'll be all right with Lucilla,' he replied. 'You'd better go back to the others before Dan or Lou gets back. Thanks for coming with me, Julian. You're a pal.'

Julian walked back up the hill to the others, feeling very sorry for poor Ned. What a life he had with Dan and Lou.

Go to **121**.

125

'Ned! We're going to the town for the day!' shouted Julian at the top of his voice. 'We're . . .'

Tiger Dan suddenly appeared behind Ned and grabbed his arm fiercely. Ned put up a hand to protect his face, as if he expected a blow. Julian shouted again:

'We're going into the town, Ned! We won't be back until evening. Can you hear me? WE'RE GOING TO THE TOWN!'

The whole camp must have heard Julian. He was quite determined that, whoever else didn't hear, Tiger Dan certainly should.

Ned tried to shake off his uncle's hand, and opened his mouth to shout something back. Dan put his hand across Ned's mouth and pulled him away.

'HOW'S BARKER?' shouted Julian, but Ned had disappeared, dragged into his uncle's caravan by Dan. The little elephant man heard, however.

'Barker's not too bad,' he said. 'Lucilla's a wonder with sick animals.'

The children were all pleased to hear that Barker was getting better, and set off for the bus stop feeling much more cheerful. Dick looked round to see if anyone was watching them.

Go to **130**.

126

'George and I found something that looks like the mouth of a cave,' said Dick excitedly. 'I left her there and came back to tell you.'

'Come on,' said Julian. 'Let's go and have a look.'

Dick led Julian and Anne across the heather roughly in the direction of the farm. He turned down a small track, and Julian and Anne could see a rocky outcrop not far away, with George and Timmy standing beside it.

'Come and look at this, you two!' George shouted.

When they reached the rocks, George showed them what looked like the mouth of a small cave. It was quite low, and covered with matted weeds. George pushed the weeds aside, and Julian bent down and peered inside.

'It certainly looks like a cave,' he said. 'Luckily I put my torch in my pocket – we always seem to need torches on our adventures! I'm going to go in and have a look round.'

Bending almost double, he disappeared into the mouth of the cave. The others waited anxiously outside.

Go to **128**.

127

Timmy didn't bark any more. He slept quietly, with one ear cocked. Julian lay in bed and thought hard. Probably Dan and Lou had come creeping up in the dark, hoping that Timmy had eaten the meat and been poisoned. But when they heard him bark, they knew he was all right, and they must have gone away again.

'There's something behind all this,' Julian thought, 'but what can it be? *Why* do they want us out of this particular spot?'

He couldn't imagine. A vague plan began to form in his mind. Perhaps they could make Dan and Lou believe that they had all gone off for the day? But really he, Julian, would be left behind, in hiding, and maybe he could find out something, if Lou and Dan came along.

Julian fell asleep in the middle of thinking out his plan.

Go to **131**.

128

'Do you suppose he's got stuck?' asked Anne, after a while.

George shook her head.

'I don't think so,' she said. 'He'll be very careful. He always is!'

As she spoke, Julian wriggled out of the entrance to the cave. He was covered in earth and bits of grass, and there was a muddy streak on one of his cheeks.

'Well?' said Dick and George together.

Julian got to his feet and started to brush himself off.

'It's not really a cave at all,' he told them. 'There's a little passage that's so low I had to get down on my stomach and wriggle along, but it comes to a dead end. I did find something, though. This!'

Julian put his hand in his pocket and pulled out a large, rusted iron key. They all bent over to examine it.

'It could be important,' said George.

'Or it could have been there for years and years,' said Dick.

'Either way,' said Julian, 'I don't think this place has been used by Dan and Lou. It's just some kind of burrow.'

'What shall we do now?' asked George, as they walked back to the caravans.

Go to **133**.

They watched Ned and Pongo for a little while, and then the little boat drew into the shore.

Julian called everyone together and put forward the plan he had been thinking out the night before.

'I'd like to find out what there is about this place that attracts Lou and Dan,' he said. 'There's *something* not far from here that makes the men want to get rid of us. Now, suppose we four and Timmy go off down the hill, passing the camp, and we yell out to Ned that we're *all* going to the town for the day – and you three do go, but I slip back up the hill and hide. If Dan and Lou come up here, I shall be able to see what they're up to!'

'That's a good idea,' said George. 'Let's get ready right now.'

Anne was looking thoughtful. 'Supposing . . .' she said. 'Supposing Lou and Tiger Dan had a hiding-place up here. Somewhere they kept secret things. They wouldn't be able to get to it when we were around, would they?'

'Right! And they'd be afraid we might find it ourselves!' added Dick excitedly. 'I think we should have a look.'

'Good thinking,' said Julian. 'Let's all go a different way. Come on!'

If you think they find something, go to 135.
If not, go to 140.

130

'Lou the acrobat is watching us,' he said. 'Good! Can he see the bus stop from where he is?'

Julian turned round. 'Yes, he can. He'll watch to see us all get into the bus - so I'd better climb in too, and I'll get out at the first stop, double back, and get into the hills by some path he won't be able to see.'

'Right,' said Dick, enjoying the thought of playing

a trick on Lou. 'Come on, there's the bus. We'll have to run for it!'

They all got into the bus. Lou was still watching, a small figure very far away. Dick felt inclined to wave cheekily to him, but didn't.

They climbed aboard the bus, and Julian got off at the first stop.

'Well, I'll see you this evening,' he said. 'Send Timmy on ahead to the caravans when you come back – just in case the men are anywhere about. I may not be able to warn you.'

'Right,' said Dick. 'Goodbye – and good luck!'

Go to **134**.

131

The next morning was not so warm, and the sky was cloudy. Nobody was very cheerful, because they kept thinking of Ned and poor Barker. They ate their breakfast almost in silence, and then began to stack the plates, ready to take them to the spring for washing.

'*I'll* go to the farm this morning,' said Julian. 'You sit on the ledge with the binoculars, Dick. We'll see if Ned goes out in his boat and waves. I've an idea that he won't want us down at the camp this morning. If he suspects Dan and Lou of putting down the meat that made Barker ill, he'll probably have had a horrible row with them.'

He went off to the farm with two empty baskets. Mrs Mackie was ready for him, and he bought a further supply of delicious food. As a present, she gave Julian a round ginger cake, warm from the oven.

'Do the circus folk ever come here to buy food?' Julian asked, as he paid Mrs Mackie.

'They do come sometimes,' said Mrs Mackie. 'I can't abide the men. There were two here last year, messing about in the hills, that my husband had to send off quick.'

Julian pricked up his ears. 'Two men? What were they like?'

'Nasty-looking chaps,' replied Mrs Mackie. 'Bad-
tempered, both of them. They came up here at
night, and we were afraid our chickens would go.
They swore they weren't after our chickens – but
what else would they be here at night for?'

'I can't imagine,' said Julian. He was sure that
the two men Mrs Mackie spoke of were Lou and
Tiger Dan. Why did they wander about in the
hills at night?

'Thanks, Mrs Mackie,' he said. 'Goodbye.'

He set off back to the camp, looking very thoughtful.

Go to **122**.

132

Julian lay quite still, watching the lake, and keeping his eyes and ears open for anyone coming up the hill. He could see spires of smoke rising from where the circus camp lay, far below. He saw a couple of boats on the lake – people fishing, he supposed. He saw some rabbits playing on the hillside.

The sun came out from behind the clouds for about ten minutes, and Julian began to feel uncomfortably hot. Then it went in again and he felt better.

Then, suddenly, he heard someone whistling. He stiffened himself in expectation. Was it Dan or Lou?

If you think it's Dan or Lou, go to **137**.

If you think it's someone else, go to **143**.

133

If you have arrived from **128**, *score* ◯ ◯ ◯.

'Let's put our plan into action,' said Julian promptly. 'Let the men themselves show us what they're after. We'll go down the hill, and yell out to Ned that we're off for the day – and hope that Lou and Tiger Dan will hear us!'

The four of them set off down the hill with Timmy. As they walked, Julian and Dick discussed what they should do.

'Have lunch in the town,' suggested Julian. 'Keep away for the whole day, if you can, to give the men a chance to come up the hill. Perhaps you could buy some tinned fruit – it would make a change.'

'Right,' said Dick, 'but be careful. I don't think those two men would stop at much.'

They were now at the bottom of the hill, near the circus camp. The children could hear the barking of the dogs and the shrill trumpeting of Old Lady the elephant. They looked for Ned, but unfortunately there was no sign of him. It wouldn't be any good setting off to the town if they couldn't tell Ned they were going!

Nobody dared to go into the camp, remembering the red cloths that Ned and Pongo had waved. They all stood still for a moment, not sure what to do, then Julian opened his mouth and yelled:

'Ned! Ned!'

No answer and no Ned. The elephant man heard him shouting and came up.

'Do you want Ned?' he asked. 'I'll fetch him.'

'Thanks,' said Julian.

The little man went off, whistling, and soon Ned appeared from behind a caravan, looking rather scared. He didn't come near Julian, but stood a good way away, looking pale and rather worried.

Go to **125**.

Julian waved to the others and set off back down the road towards the circus camp. He was hoping to find a path that would take him up into the hills and back to the caravans. Before he had walked very far, he found a track running off to his right, and he decided to take it. As he walked along he thought about Lou and Dan, and their strange behaviour, and a shiver of excitement went down his spine. Perhaps today he would find out what was going on!

After he had been walking for about ten minutes, he came to a place where the path, which had been sloping gently uphill for some time, divided, going round either side of the hill.

Julian stood still, trying to make up his mind which path to take: the left-hand one, or the right-hand one.

If you think he should turn left, go to **139**.
If you think he should turn right, go to **144**.

'Wait a minute,' said George. 'I don't think it would be a good idea all to go off in different directions. We might come face-to-face with Dan and Lou!'

'Yes, I think you're right, George,' said Julian. 'George, why don't you and Dick go together, and Anne can come with me.' He looked at his watch. 'It's half past nine now. We'll search for half an hour, then meet back here. OK?'

They split up into pairs to search. Timmy went with George, of course, and thoroughly enjoyed himself exploring every rabbit hole he found.

'Just what are we looking for?' Anne asked Julian as they walked away from the caravans.

'I'm not quite sure,' he replied. 'A cave – or something like that – some kind of hiding-place. I'm sure we'll know it if we find it.'

Go to **123**.

Julian decided to take the right fork. It seemed to him that the left fork would take him back in the direction of the road, and that was the last thing he wanted. He was getting worried he might miss Dan and Lou if he didn't get back to the campsite soon, or worse still, arrive back to find they were already there!

The path ran along the side of the hill, and Julian was sure he was going in the right direction this time. Sure enough, before long he came to a place where the path he was on was joined by one coming from the left. He stopped and looked to his left, and he could see the road, and the stop where he had got off the bus.

'If I go straight on now, I'm sure I'll be all right,' he thought, and set off again.

Go to **142**.

*If you have arrived from **143**, score* ◯◁ .

For a moment or two there was quiet, then Julian heard a harsh voice that he recognised. It was Tiger Dan, and with him was Lou. The two of them came right into the hollow, and Julian heard them talking.

'Yes, there's nobody here. Those kids have gone off for the day – and taken that wretched dog with them!' said Dan.

'I told you they 'ad,' growled Lou. 'There'll be nobody here all day. We can get what we want to.'

'Right then,' replied Dan.

Julian waited to see where they would go, but they didn't go out of the hollow. They stayed there, apparently beside the caravans. Julian didn't dare look over the edge of the roof to see what they were up to. Then a strange scuffling sound began, and he could hear the men panting. The caravan on which Julian was lying began to shake a little.

Go to **141**.

138

Julian walked on, feeling a bit shaken after his fall. With an effort he stopped thinking about the mysterious man on the chestnut horse and, instead, turned his mind to his plans for hiding. He would have to take some food into his hiding-place with him, because he might be there for a long time. It was lucky it wasn't too hot today, otherwise he might be very uncomfortable.

Just as he was beginning to wonder if he had taken the wrong fork, he came to a place where the path he was using was joined by another one coming in from the left.

'That's the path I came up from the bus stop,' he said to himself. 'So if I keep straight on, I ought to be all right. Thank goodness for that! I feel as though I've been walking for hours.'

Go to **142**.

139

Julian decided to turn left. In a little while the path began to climb the hill quite steeply, and Julian hoped it would take him directly to the spot where the caravans were parked.

He walked along as quickly as he could. He was rather worried that he might already have missed Lou and Dan, or that he would stumble on them snooping around the caravans. He also tried to think of a good hiding-place. It would have to be somewhere he could hide for a long time, without getting too uncomfortable. He had better take some sandwiches and cake into his hiding-place, too.

Go to **142**.

They separated and went off, George and Timmy together, of course. They hunted in the hillside for possible caves, or any kind of hiding-place. Timmy put his head down every rabbit hole and felt very busy indeed.

After about half an hour the others heard Julian shouting. They ran back to the caravans, sure that he had found something exciting.

But he hadn't. He had simply got tired of hunting and decided to give it up. He shook his head when they rushed up to him, asking what he had found.

'Nothing,' he said. 'I'm fed up with looking. There's not a cave anywhere here, I'm sure of that. Anyone else found anything?'

'Not a thing,' said everyone in disappointment. 'What shall we do now?'

Go to **133**.

'What *are* they doing?' thought Julian in bewilderment. He slid quietly to the edge of the caravan roof and cautiously peeped over. There was nobody on the ground on that side of the caravan. He slid carefully across and looked over the other side of the caravan, but there was nobody there either!

'They must be *underneath* the caravan,' thought Julian, going back to the middle of the roof. 'Underneath! Why?'

It was quite impossible to see underneath the caravan from where he was, so he had to lie quietly and wonder what the men were doing. They grunted and groaned, and seemed to be scrabbling about, but nothing happened. Then Julian heard them scrambling out from underneath, angry and disappointed.

'I'm fed up with this,' said Lou in a disagreeable voice. 'We'll have to shift this van. Those tiresome kids! What did they want to choose this spot for?'

Then Julian got a shock! The caravan he was on began to move. Were the men going to push it over the ledge and down the hillside?

He was suddenly very scared. He wondered if he had better slide off the roof and run. He wouldn't have much chance if the caravan went hurtling down the hill! On the other hand, he shuddered to think what might happen if the men saw him running away. Desperately he tried to make up his mind what to do.

If you think Julian should jump off the caravan, go to **147**.
If you think he should hang on, go to **151**.

142

If you have arrived from **136**, *score* ↻.
If you have arrived from **138**, *score* ↻ ↻ ↻.

The path led Julian not very far from the Mackies'

farm, so he knew where he was. As soon as he got back to the caravans he made himself some sandwiches, cut some cake, and also packed some plums that Mrs Mackie had sent. He put the food together in a neat parcel, then went outside to find a hiding-place.

There were no trees near enough, and the surrounding bushes were all gorse, which was much too prickly. Suddenly he had a brainwave.

'I'll climb on to the roof of one of the caravans!' he thought. 'Nobody will be able to see me – and no one would ever think of looking up there. I'll have a good view of the men wherever they go!'

It wasn't very easy to climb on to the high roof. He had to get one of the horse's reins, loop it at the end, and lasso the chimney in order to climb up.

He threw his packet of food on to the roof and then scrambled up. He pulled up the rein, and then lay down flat. He was certain that nobody could see him from below. Of course, if the men went higher up the hill and looked down on the caravans, he could be spotted – but he would have to chance that.

Go to **132**.

143

Julian lay on top of the caravan, hardly daring to breathe. Very cautiously he peeped over the edge. He could still hear whistling, getting louder and louder, but he couldn't see anyone. Then he saw a figure walking down the hill, some distance away. It was one of the men from Mr Mackie's farm – Julian had seen him in the fields once or twice. Julian relaxed again.

After a while he began to get bored. The rabbits had gone in, and not even a butterfly flew past. He could see no birds except a yellowhammer that sat on the top spray of a bush, singing cheerfully. Suddenly it gave a cry of alarm and flew off. Something had startled it. Julian heard something too, and glued his eyes to the track that led up the hill. His heart started to thump. He could see two men. Were they Tiger Dan and Lou?

Go to **137**.

144

Julian decided to turn right, and set off again. The path wound along the side of the hill, and it was rather overgrown and difficult to follow. Obviously it didn't get much use. He was glad that it wasn't as hot and sunny today, otherwise he would have been getting rather uncomfortable.

'The most important thing is to find somewhere really safe to hide,' he said to himself. 'There mustn't be any chance of Lou or Dan seeing me – I don't want to have to tangle with those two on my own!'

Julian was so busy thinking about where he might hide that he hadn't been paying much attention to where he was going, and suddenly he realised that he was back at the road again! The path had skirted the edge of the hill, then curved back down to join the road.

'Oh, no!' he muttered crossly. 'Now I'll have to go back the way I came, and I've wasted quite a lot of time. Oh, BOTHER!'

He turned round and started to walk back the way he had come, but before long he had to stop again. Once again the path divided, but instead of one path going straight on, and one to the left, as he had expected, it forked right and left.

'This doesn't look like the place where I turned the wrong way,' he said to himself. '*Now* which way should I go?'

If you think he should take the left fork, go to **149**.
If you think he should take the right fork, go to **136**.

If you have arrived from **150***, score* ◯◁.

The men were now scrabbling away again by the back steps of the caravan. Julian was absolutely eaten up with curiosity, but he didn't dare move. He could find out the secret when the men had gone. Meanwhile, he really must be patient or he would spoil everything.

There was some muttered talking, but Julian couldn't catch a word. Then, quite suddenly, there was complete and utter silence. Not a word. Not a pant or even a grunt. Nothing at all.

Julian lay still. He thought the men might still be there, and he didn't want to give himself away. He lay for quite a long time, waiting and wondering, but he heard nothing.

Then he saw a robin fly to a nearby bramble spray. It flicked its wings and looked about. A rabbit popped out of a hole on the hillside and capered about, running suddenly up to the hollow.

'Well,' thought Julian, 'it's plain the men aren't here now, or the birds and animals wouldn't be about like this. Those men have gone somewhere – though goodness knows where. I think I can take a look now.'

Go to **148**.

146

Round a curve in the track came a large chestnut horse, moving extremely fast. Julian had to jump out of its way, otherwise he would have been knocked down as the animal galloped past. He just had time to see that the horse was ridden by a very fair man, and Julian caught the flash of his chilly blue eyes as he vanished down the path.

Julian had had to jump out of the way so quickly that he had fallen over, so he picked himself up and rubbed his elbow.

'Whoever was riding that horse had no business

to be going that fast. If I hadn't got out of the way in time, I might have been killed!' he muttered angrily. 'I've grazed my elbow, too.'

He searched in his pockets until he found his handkerchief, which he wound round his elbow, pulling the knot tight with his teeth.

'There,' he thought, 'that will have to do until I've got time to have another look at it. Now I must get back to the caravans.'

Go to **138**.

147

Julian decided to jump off the roof of the caravan. The men were at one end, pushing, so if he jumped off the other end he would be able to dash across the hollow and hide on the far side of the other caravan. The men were making quite a lot of noise as they pushed, and with any luck they wouldn't hear him.

He eased himself to the end of the caravan, then wriggled feet first over the edge and dropped to the ground. He landed with a thump, then saw to his horror that the rein he had used to lasso the chimney was still there, hanging down the side of the caravan. Supposing they saw it? His forehead wet and his hands shaking, Julian flattened himself against the caravan as it moved slowly towards the ledge, wondering whether he could safely make a dash across to the other caravan.

Just then he heard a voice.

'Hey!' said Lou.

Go to **150**.

148

He slid round and peered over the end of the caravan. Looking down at the ground there was absolutely nothing to tell him what the men had been doing, or where they had gone. The heather grew as luxuriantly there as it did everywhere else.

'This really is very strange,' said Julian to himself. 'The men have certainly gone – vanished into thin air, apparently. Dare I explore a bit? No, I'd better not. The men might reappear at any minute, and they'll be furious if they find me.'

The sun came out, and Julian got hotter and hotter as he lay there. He wished the men would reappear and go down the hill back to the circus camp. He was terribly sleepy. He yawned, and his eyelids drooped.

Go to **153**.

149

Julian decided to take the left fork. The right fork went straight along for a few metres, then seemed to turn down the hill, and Julian was afraid he would end up back at the road again, and that was the last thing he wanted. He was worried that he might miss Dan and Lou if he didn't get back to the caravans soon, or worse still, arrive back to find they were already there!

He plodded steadily on. He could see the road, away to his left, with cars moving along, their windscreens glittering in the occasional gleams of sunshine that broke through the clouds.

All at once he heard a noise, as if something or somebody was coming towards him along the track – coming very fast. The next moment he saw what it was.

Go to **146**.

150

Julian froze. Lou had seen him!

'Hey!' said Lou again. 'Don't push it down the hill!'

Julian nearly collapsed with relief. Lou hadn't seen him after all. He had been talking to Tiger Dan!

Julian waited to be sure that the caravan had stopped moving, then he grabbed the rein and scrambled back up to the roof, praying they wouldn't hear him.

'What was that?' said Tiger Dan nervously.

Lou chuckled. 'You're jumpy today, aren't you? I told you – there's no one around. Let's get on with it.'

As Julian lay there, he thought over what Lou and Dan had done. Obviously they didn't mean to destroy the caravan, only to move it to get at something underneath. But what could it be? He racked his brains to try and remember what the floor of the hollow had been like when Dobby and Trotter pulled the caravans into it. As far as he could recall it was just an ordinary heathery hollow.

Go to **145**.

151

Julian decided to stay on the caravan roof. He clung to the chimney with both hands, whilst the men shoved hard against the caravan. It ran a few feet to the rocky ledge, and then stopped. Julian felt his forehead getting very damp, and he saw that his hands were trembling. He felt ashamed of being so scared, but he couldn't help it.

'Hey! Don't send it down the hill!' said Lou in

alarm, and Julian's heart felt lighter. So they didn't mean to destroy the caravan, only move it to get at something underneath. But what could it be? Julian racked his brains to try and remember what the floor of the hollow had been like when Dobby and Trotter pulled the caravans into it. As far as he could remember it was just an ordinary heathery hollow.

Go to **145**.

152

Julian stared in astonishment. It was Pongo! He had obviously followed Ned up the hill, and had seen Dan and Lou threatening the boy.

Pongo flung himself on the men and bit Lou's arm hard. Then he bit Dan's leg. The men both yelled loudly, and Lou lashed out with his foot. It caught Pongo on the shoulder. The chimpanzee made a shrill chattering noise, and leapt on Lou with his arms open, clasping the man to him, trying to bite his throat. Lou yelled to Ned.

'Call him off! He'll kill me!'

'Pongo!' shouted Ned. 'Stop it! Pongo! Come here!'

The chimpanzee gave Lou a last nip and let him go. Lou dropped to the ground, rubbing his arm and glaring at Ned.

'Just you wait till I get you back to the circus,' he growled at Ned. 'I'll give you what for, you and that dratted chimp!'

Suddenly a dog barked, and Julian grinned to himself in relief. He knew that bark!

Go to **157**.

153

How long he had slept Julian had no idea, but he woke with a jump. Just in time, he grabbed the chimney, to stop himself slipping off as the caravan was being jerked into place.

'We might as well sit down and have something to eat,' said Dan's voice. 'We can sit over there on that ledge.'

'Good idea,' replied Lou.

Julian groaned silently. If Lou and Dan were going to have something to eat, they would be there for at least another half an hour, and he was getting very uncomfortable on the caravan roof. He could hear the men eating, and talking in low voices. Then there was silence, which lasted so long that Julian wondered if they had gone. Very cautiously he raised his head and looked towards the ledge. Lou and Dan were lying flat on their backs, fast asleep!

Julian sat up with relief and stretched himself. He could see two strong sacks lying beside the men. Julian was sure that Dan and Lou hadn't had sacks with them when they arrived.

Just then, he heard someone coming up the track, and he saw that it was Ned. Ned caught sight of Julian, and seemed about to call out. Julian shook his head frantically, and pointed, to try and warn him. He was going to walk straight into Dan and Lou!

If you think Ned heeds Julian's warning, go to **158**.
If you think he ignores him, go to **163**.

154

If you have arrived from **165**, *score* ᠭ᠋ ᠭ᠋.
If you have arrived from **175**, *score* ᠭ᠋ ᠭ᠋ ᠭ᠋ ᠭ᠋ ᠭ᠋.

Julian had pulled up a small patch of heather, and underneath they could see what looked like branches.

The children went on pulling up the heather until they had cleared a patch about two metres square. A number of wooden planks were laid neatly side by side.

'Let's pull them up!' said George.

They pulled up the planks one by one and piled them on one side. Then they saw that they had uncovered the entrance to a deep hole.

'I'll get my torch,' said Julian.

He fetched it and, turning it on, flashed it down the hole. The light showed them a dark opening, going down into the hillside, with footholds sticking out of one side. They all stood and looked down in excitement.

'To think we went and put our caravan *exactly* over the entrance of the men's hiding place!' said Dick. 'No wonder they were wild! No wonder they changed their minds and told us we could go down to the lake and camp there instead!'

'So that's where the men went!' said Julian, staring into the hole. Where does it lead to? They were down there a very long time.'

Go to **166**.

*If you have arrived from **161**, score* ⌒⌒ .

'No! No!' said poor Ned. 'I've only just come. I've been at the camp all morning, helping Larry and Rossy with the horses.'

'I don't believe you,' said Dan, in a cold, hard voice that sent shivers down Julian's spine. 'I'm going to box your ears so hard you won't never forget it. Perhaps that'll teach you not to spy on us.'

'I wasn't spying on you,' said Ned, trying to pull away from Dan's hard hands.

Julian decided that he must try and rescue Ned. He didn't want to give away the fact that he had been spying, nor did he want to fight the two men, for he was certain that he would get the worst of it, but he had to try and help Ned. He was just about to jump on Dan when a black, furry bundle came bounding into the hollow and flung itself on the man.

Go to **152**.

'Please let me come, Julian,' pleaded Dick.

'All right then,' said his brother. 'Come on!'

Ned went down the hole first, followed by Julian, then Dick. Anne and George knelt by the hole, George looking rather envious, and Anne looking very relieved. She had no wish to start climbing down into dark holes!

'Pongo!' yelled Ned as he climbed down. 'Pongo! Come here, you silly chimp!'

Pongo had not gone very far. He didn't like the dark down there very much, and he came to Ned as soon as he saw the light of the torch. At the bottom of the hole the three boys found themselves in a narrow passage, which widened as they went further into the hill.

Go to **164**.

Timmy ran into the clearing, barking at the top of his voice. It was too much for Dan and Lou. They got to their feet and ran off down the hill as fast as they could go. Ned sat down abruptly, because his legs were shaking so much that he thought he would fall over!

The sound of voices could be heard coming up the hill, and a moment later George, Dick and Anne came up the track.

'Hello!' shouted Dick. 'We thought it was safe to come back, because we saw Dan and Lou running down the hill. Oh, look – there's Pongo!'

Pongo solemnly shook hands with them all, then walked round Timmy and shook hands with his tail, which made them laugh.

'Well, did anything happen, Julian?' asked George.

'Yes,' answered Julian, 'quite a lot. Let's get something to drink and I'll tell you all about it.'

Go to **162**.

Ned blinked, and stared at Julian, who shook his head even harder. At last Ned realised that something was wrong. He moved off the track and disappeared. Julian thought that he must have decided to go back to the camp, but a few minutes later Ned appeared from the far side of the little hollow, and moved silently towards Julian's caravan.

'Go back into the trees!' Julian called, as loudly as he dared. 'I'll come and join you. Dan and Lou are here, but they're asleep.'

Ned nodded, and moved back into the trees, out of sight. Julian slid cautiously down from his hiding-place, and ran quickly to join him.

'What's up?' asked Ned.

'Dan and Lou are there, asleep,' repeated Julian. 'The others have gone into the town, but I only pretended to go with them. I got off at the first bus stop, walked back here, and hid. I wanted to see if Dan and Lou came up here while they thought there was no one around.'

'I heard Dan and Lou talking about you lot having gone to the town,' said Ned. 'I didn't know they were planning to come up here, though.'

Go to **168**.

159

They all finished their drinks, and then Julian got up.

'And now,' he said, 'let's do a little exploring and find out where the men went, shall we?'

'Oh, yes!' said George, who had sat still quite long enough. 'We *must* find out! Do we have to get under the caravan, Julian?'

''Fraid so,' said Julian. 'You sit here, Ned, and keep guard in case Lou or Dan come back.'

He didn't think for a moment that they would, but he could see that Ned needed to sit quietly for a while. Ned, however, had different ideas. He was going to share this adventure!

'Timmy's guard enough, and so is Pongo,' he said. 'They'll hear anyone coming half a mile away. I'm in on this.'

And he was. He went scrabbling underneath the low-slung base of the caravan with the others, eager to find out anything he could. Unfortunately they soon found that they couldn't explore down in the heather with the caravan base just above their heads. They would have to move it.

It took all five of them to move the caravan a few metres. Then they dropped down on to the thick carpet of heather again.

They all groped round, pulling at tufts of heather to see if they came up easily. Suddenly Julian gave a shout.

'Hey! Look at this!'

At the same time George gave a yell.

'Look what I've found!'

If you want to see what Julian has found, go to **154**.
If you want to see what George has found, go to **170**.

193

The piece of string was very dirty, and in places it was worn down to a few strands, but George was able to pull it up quite easily – until suddenly it stopped moving! She gave another tug, but nothing happened.

'I can't pull it any further,' she said. 'It feels as though there's something stuck down the hole. What shall we do?'

'Can you get your hand into the hole and feel around?' suggested Ned.

'I'll try,' said George. 'Here, you hold the string, Anne, and I'll put my hand down the hole.'

Anne took the string, and George slid her hand into the hole. She had to lie flat on her stomach so that she could push her arm in right up to her shoulder. She wriggled her hand around, but could only feel the piece of string, which was stretched taut.

George pulled her arm out of the rabbit hole and sat up.

'I can't feel anything,' she said, 'but the string is pulled tight, so there *must* be something on the other end of it. What shall we do?'

Go to **167**.

161

Unfortunately for Ned, as he went down the path he tripped and went sprawling. Without thinking he gave a yell, and Lou and Dan both woke up! They sat up, and saw Ned at once.

'Here! You come here!' yelled Dan, and Ned dared not disobey. The men glared at him, and he began to tremble.

'I didn't know you were here, honest!' said poor Ned. 'I only came up to look for my knife that I lost yesterday!'

Dan shook him hard.

'How long have you been here? You been spying on us?'

Go to **155**.

162

Julian told the others about his day, and how he had hidden on the caravan roof. He described how the men had arrived, and gone under the caravan and then moved it. Then Ned told his part of the story.

'Dan and Lou mean to make you move from here,' he concluded, 'and they're not too fussy about how they do it. You're going to have to be very careful. Keep an eye on Timmy, and don't leave the caravans for too long. I daren't go back to the circus now,' he said. 'I don't know what those two might do to me if I go back!'

'Don't worry, Ned,' said Julian. 'You're not going back to the circus, you're going to stay here with us. We're happy to have you, aren't we?' he added, looking round at the others.

They all nodded in agreement. Ned grinned all over his face.

'Thanks!' he said.

Go to **159**.

163

Ned didn't understand. He grinned and, to Julian's horror, began to climb up the hillside to the rocky ledge! The men were sleeping there, and Julian saw with dismay that Ned would probably heave himself right up on top of them.

'Look out!' he said, in a low, urgent voice. 'Look out, Ned!'

But it was too late. Ned hauled himself up on to the ledge and, to his utter horror, found himself sprawling on top of Dan. He gave a yell and tried to slide away – but Dan, rousing suddenly, shot out a hand and grabbed him.

Lou woke up too. The men glared at poor Ned,

and the boy began to tremble.

'I didn't know you were here, I swear it!' he said. 'I only came up to look for my knife that I lost yesterday!'

Dan shook him hard.

'How long have you been here? You been spying on us?'

Go to **155**.

164

'Must be caves somewhere,' said Julian, flashing his torch round. 'We know that a lot of springs run out of this hill. I'll bet that through the centuries the water has eaten away the softer rock, and left caves and tunnels everywhere under the hill. And somewhere in a cave Lou and Dan store away things they don't want anyone to know about. Stolen goods, I should think.'

They made their way along the passage, Pongo

sticking close behind Ned. He didn't like this dark, mysterious place. Dick tagged along behind. He could hardly see a thing, because the torch was so far in front of him. Suddenly he tripped over a rock in the floor of the passage and went sprawling.

'Julian!' he called. 'Julian, I'll have to go back. I really can't see a thing. You two go on without me.'

'All right, Dick,' said Julian. 'Can you find your way back to the hole?'

'Yes,' answered Dick. 'I can just see a faint patch of light. I'll be fine.'

He turned back towards the hole, and Ned and Julian went on down the passage.

Go to **169**.

165

It was a very dirty piece of string, frayed and worn almost through in places. George pulled and pulled, and eventually the end of the string appeared. There was nothing attached to it.

'Oh, darn!' said George in disgust.

'Never mind,' said Julian. 'It was worth investigating. Come on, let's have a look at the place that I found.'

In their excitement over the piece of string, they had forgotten that Julian had also found something interesting, and now they all ran over to have a look.

Go to **154**.

166

Pongo suddenly took it in to his head to go down the hole. Down he went, feeling for the footholds with his hairy feet, grinning up at the others. He disappeared at the bottom. Julian's torch couldn't pick him out at all.

'Hey, Pongo! Don't lose yourself down there!' called Ned anxiously. But Pongo had gone.

'Darn him!' said Ned. 'He'll never find his way back if he goes wandering about underground. I'll have to go and find him. Can I have your torch, Julian?'

'I'll come too,' said Julian. 'George, get me your torch as well, will you please?'

'It's broken,' said George. 'I dropped it last night, and nobody else has got one.'

'What a nuisance!' exclaimed Julian. 'I want us to go and explore down there, but we can't with only one torch. Well, I'll just go down with Ned and get Pongo – have a quick look round and then come back. I may see something worth seeing!'

'Can't I come too?' asked Dick. 'I'm longing to know what's down there!'

Julian hesitated.

If you think Julian should let Dick go with them, go to **156**.

If you think he should say no, go to **171**.

167

'I think we'd better dig down and see if we can find the end of the string,' said Julian.

'How are we going to dig?' asked Anne. 'We haven't got a spade, have we?'

'No, but I did bring a trowel,' said George. 'I thought we might have to dig holes to bury rubbish, or something like that. I'll go and get it.'

She disappeared into the girls' caravan and

came out a moment later clutching a small trowel.

'It's going to take rather a long time if that's all we've got to dig with,' grumbled Dick.

George was tired after their day in the town, and hungry too. She lost her temper.

'Well, if you've got a better idea. I'd like to hear it!' she snapped, and, throwing the trowel on the ground at Dick's feet, she rushed into her caravan and slammed the door.

'Now look what you've done, Dick!' shouted Anne, and ran after George.

Go to **172**.

168

'Why did you come up here, Ned?' asked Julian. 'We told you we wouldn't be here.'

'I lost my knife,' explained Ned. 'I thought I might have left it up here, and I come up to look for it, see?'

'Well, perhaps you'd better go back to the circus camp, and we'll look for your knife when the others come back,' suggested Julian. 'I don't think Dan and Lou will be very pleased if they wake up and find you here.'

'Too right they won't,' said Ned. 'What are you going to do, though?'

'I'll just have to climb back on the roof of the caravan and wait until they wake up and go,' answered Julian. 'I don't think they'll want to hang around in case we – or at least the others – find them. Bye, Ned! See you later!'

Ned disappeared, and a moment later Julian, back on the roof of the caravan, saw him going down the track.

Go to **161**.

169

*If you have arrived from **164**, score* ⌒.

The passage ended in a small cave that seemed to have no other opening out of it at all. There was nothing in it. Julian flashed his torch up and down the walls.

He saw footholds up one part, and traced them to a hole in the roof, which must have been made, years before, by running water.

'That's the way we go!' he said. 'Come on!'

'Wait!' said Ned. 'Isn't your torch getting rather faint?'

'Yes you're right,' replied Julian in alarm, and shook his torch violently to make the light brighter. The battery was almost flat, however, and no better light came. Instead the light grew fainter, until it was just a pin-prick in the torch.

'Come on – we'd better get back at once,' said Julian, feeling a bit scared. 'I don't want to wander about here in the pitch dark. Not my idea of fun at all.'

Ned took a firm hold of Pongo's hairy paw, and an equally firm hold of Julian's jumper. He didn't want to lose either of them! Just then, the light in the torch went out completely. Now they had to find their way back in absolute darkness!

Go to **173**.

170

George sounded so excited that even Julian rushed to see what she'd found.

She had pulled up several handfuls of heather, and underneath was what looked like a rabbit hole. There was nothing particularly unusual about finding a rabbit hole, but this one had a long piece of string trailing out of it!

'Do you think there's something on the other end of that string?' asked Anne in excitement.

'Well, I can't imagine why anyone would push a

piece of string down a rabbit hole just for the fun of it,' said George.

'A rabbit might have found it and pulled it back to the hole,' argued Dick.

'Just pull the string, George,' said Julian, 'then we can see if there is anything tied to the other end.'

George started to pull.

If you think there's something on the end of the string, go to **160**. *If not, go to* **165**.

171

Julian shook his head.

'I think it would be better if you stayed here with Anne and George,' he said, 'just in case something happens.'

'OK,' said Dick, looking rather disappointed.

Ned went down the hole first, and Julian followed. The others all knelt round the hole, watching enviously. When Julian and Ned had disappeared, they sat back to wait.

'Pongo!' yelled Ned as he climbed down. 'Pongo! Come here, you silly chimp!'

Pongo had not gone very far. He didn't like the dark down there very much, and he came to Ned as soon as he saw the light of the torch. At the bottom of the hole the boys found themselves in a narrow passage, which widened as they went further into the hill.

'Must be caves somewhere,' said Julian, flashing his torch round. 'We know that a lot of springs run out of this hill. I'll bet that through the centuries the water has eaten away the softer rock and left caves and tunnels everywhere under the hill. And somewhere in a cave Lou and Dan store away things they don't want anyone to know about.'

Go to **169**.

Dick looked at Ned and Julian in amazement.

'What on earth made George fly off the handle like that?' he asked. 'I only said it would take us a long time to dig with that little trowel.'

'You know how quick-tempered George is, Dick,' said Julian. 'She's probably just tired and hungry. She's worried about Timmy, too, after what happened to Barker.'

Just then the caravan door opened and Anne and George appeared, George still looking rather sulky.

'Sorry,' said Dick, and gave George's shoulder a squeeze.

George gave a rather unwilling grin.

'Me too,' she said and, picking up the trowel, she started to dig.

It did take a long time to make the rabbit hole large enough, but at last they were able to pull on the string and feel it move again. The last bit came out with a rush, and tied to the end was a rusty tin box! It was small and square, and looked like a cash box. It was very rusty, and they had trouble prising the lid open, but at last it was done. Inside the box was a large, rusty key!

Go to **175**.

173

Julian felt round for the beginning of the passage that led back to the hole. He found it and made his way up it, feeling the sides with his hands. It wasn't a pleasant experience, but fortunately they had not gone very far into the hill, and soon they were back at the entrance hole.

The others helped them out at the top, and Julian told them about the hole in the roof of the little cave.

'That's where the men went,' he finished, 'and tomorrow we'll go down to the town and buy torches, matches, candles and anything else we can think of that might be useful, and then come back and do a really good exploration! Things are getting exciting!'

Go to **176**.

174

Hearing George shout, the others all came running.

'What's the matter?' asked Ned. 'What's Pongo done?'

George pointed silently to the inside of the caravan. It looked as though a whirlwind had blown through it. Pongo had pulled all the clothes out of the drawers, tugged the curtains down from one of the windows, thrown the sleeping bags on the floor, and generally had a marvellous, messy time.

Ned put his hands over his face and groaned.

'Oh, Pongo!' said Anne. 'You bad chimp!'

Pongo sat on the middle of one of the bunks, holding his feet and rocking backwards and forwards. He looked so much like a naughty child that they all burst into laughter.

'Well, we obviously can't leave him here on his own,' said Ned. 'He'll wreck the place. I'll have to stay here with him.'

'Supposing Dan and Lou come up again, and find you?' said George.

Go to **186**.

175

Julian picked it up and looked at it. It was quite a modern-looking key, but so badly rusted it was clear that it had been buried down that rabbit hole for a very long time.

'Who do you suppose put it down there?' said Ned, fingering the key. 'It won't be much use – it's far too rusty to fit in a lock.'

Julian put the key in his pocket.

'We might just discover the lock that this key

fits,' he said, 'but Dan and Lou can't have been looking for it, can they, or they would have taken it away. They must have been working at the other place I found, over there.'

In their excitement over the key they had all forgotten that Julian had found something interesting, and now they all ran over to have a look.

Go to **154**.

176

Nobody disturbed them that night. Ned slept on a pile of rugs in the boys' caravan, and Pongo slept beside him. The next morning, after breakfast, they all discussed who was to go into the town.

'Not Ned and Pongo, because they wouldn't be allowed on the bus,' said Julian with a laugh. 'They'd better stay behind.'

'Not by ourselves?' asked Ned, looking alarmed. 'Suppose Lou and Uncle Dan come up? I'd be terrified, even with Pongo there.'

'It might be a better idea, Dick, if you stayed here with them,' suggested Julian.

'Couldn't we leave Pongo here on his own?' suggested George. 'We could shut him in one of the caravans, as long as we made sure that he couldn't get at any of our food!'

If you think they should leave Pongo behind on his own, go to **181**.
If you think Ned and Dick should stay behind too, go to **186**.

177

Pongo flung Dan to the ground. He made such a terrible snarling noise that Dan was terrified.

'Call him off!' he yelled. 'Lou, come and help!'

'Pongo won't obey *me*,' said Dick, still sitting down looking quite undisturbed. 'You'd better go before he bites big pieces out of you.'

Dan staggered to the rock ledge, fists raised in fury. The boy didn't move, and somehow Dan didn't dare to touch him. Pongo let him go, and stood glowering at him, his great hairy arms hanging down his sides, ready to fly at either of the men if they came near.

Tiger Dan picked up a stone – and quick as lightning Pongo flung himself on the man again and sent him rolling down the hill. Lou fled in terror. Dan got up and fled too, yelling furiously as he went. Pongo chased them in delight. He too, picked up stones and flung them with a very accurate aim, so that Dick kept hearing yells of pain.

Pongo came back, looking extremely pleased with himself. He went to the green caravan, as Dick shouted to Ned.

'All right, Ned. They've gone. Pongo and I won the battle!'

Ned came out, looking pale and rather ashamed of himself.

'Bit of a coward, aren't I?' he said. 'Leaving

you out here all alone.'

'I enjoyed it,' replied Dick truthfully, 'and so did Pongo! I enjoy having adventures – we've had quite a few, you know.'

'Really?' said Ned with interest. 'Why don't you tell me about some of them? It'll be ages before the others get back.'

So Dick began to tell the tale of all the other thrilling adventures that the five of them had had, and the time flew. Both boys were surprised when they heard Timmy barking down the track, and knew that the others were coming back.

Go to **180**.

178

The five children set off down the hill with Timmy running ahead of them, his tail wagging nineteen to the dozen. Julian had made a list of all the things he thought they ought to buy. As they walked, he put his hand in his pocket to pull out the list and check it again, but it wasn't there!

'Oh, no!' he said. 'I've left the list in the caravan.'

'Do you really need it?' asked Dick. 'Can't you remember all the things on it?'

'It's very important that we get everything on the list if we're going to be able to explore properly,' replied Julian. 'I think I'd better go back and get it. It won't take a minute.'

'We might as well all come,' said George, so they retraced their steps to the two caravans. Julian went into his to find the list, and George decided to change her jumper, since the day was warmer than she had thought. She opened the door to their caravan and gave a horrified shout.

'Pongo!'

Go to **174**.

The five of them had all tugged the van back into place the night before, in case Lou or Dan came to go down the hole again. No one could get down it while the caravan was over it. They had relaid the heather-covered planks roughly over the hole, too.

Now they had to push the caravan away from the hole again.

'Shall we push it forwards or backwards?' asked George.

A few metres in front of the caravan was a sharp drop down the hillside. Behind it was a gentle slope towards some trees.

If you think they should push the caravan forwards, go to **184**.

If you think they should push it backwards, go to **191**.

George came tearing up with Timmy at her heels.

'Are you all right? Did anything happen while we were away? Do you know, we saw Lou and Tiger Dan getting on the bus when we got off it! They were carrying bags as if they meant to go and stay somewhere.'

Ned brightened up at once. 'Did you really? Good! They came up here, you know, and Pongo chased them down the hill. They must have gone back to the camp, collected their bags, and gone to catch the bus. Good!'

'We bought good, powerful torches,' said Julian. 'Here's yours, Dick, and this one is for you, Ned.'

Ned looked rather overcome. He was not used to being given presents, the children could see.

'Look here, wouldn't it be a good time to explore underground now that we know that Lou and Dan are safely out of the way?' said Julian. 'They had bags with them, so surely that means they're going to spend the night somewhere and won't be back until tomorrow.'

'Not necessarily,' said Dick. 'They could have had anything in those bags. I vote we wait until we're sure the coast is clear.'

*If you think they should explore straight away, go to **185**.*

*If you think they should wait, go to **190**.*

181

Ned looked worried. 'I'm not sure it would be a good idea to leave Pongo here on his own,' he said. 'There's no telling what he might get up to without me.'

'Surely he'll be all right if he's shut in,' argued George. 'I expect you'd enjoy a visit to the town, Ned. Do come!'

'OK then,' said Ned. 'I'll come.'

George and Anne went into their caravan and tidied away anything that Pongo might play with,

and put things like tea and sugar away in cup-
boards. Then Ned led Pongo inside.

'You stay here, Pongo, till I get back,' he ordered.
'Don't make a mess, or misbehave, will you?'

Pongo sat down on one of the bunks and looked
at Ned reproachfully. He could tell that he was
going to be left alone, and he didn't like it! Ned
gave Pongo a pat, then came out of the caravan and
closed the door firmly.

'He'll be all right,' said Julian, seeing that Ned
still looked a bit worried. 'Come on!'

Go to **178**.

182

Ned was right. Two people were sent up to get him
– Lou and Tiger Dan. They came creeping up
through the bracken and heather, keeping a sharp
eye open for Pongo or Timmy.

Pongo sensed them long before they could be

seen and warned Ned. Ned turned pale. He was terrified of the two scoundrels.

'Get into one of the caravans,' said Dick in a low voice. 'Go on. I'll deal with those fellows – if it *is* them. Pongo will help me, if necessary.'

Ned scuttled into the green caravan and shut the door. Dick sat where he was. Pongo squatted on the roof of the caravan, watching.

Lou and Dan suddenly appeared. They saw Dick, but didn't see Pongo. They looked all round for the others.

'What do you want?' asked Dick.

'Ned and Pongo,' replied Lou with a scowl. 'Where are they?'

'They're going to stay on with us,' said Dick.

'Oh, no, they're not!' said Tiger Dan. 'Ned's in my charge, see? I'm his uncle.'

'Funny sort of uncle,' remarked Dick. 'You don't treat him very well.'

Tiger Dan went purple in the face. He looked as if he would have liked to throw Dick down the hill.

'You be careful what you say to me!' he said, beginning to shout.

Ned, hidden in the caravan, trembled when he heard Dan's angry yell. Pongo kept quite still, his face set and ugly.

'Well, you may as well say goodbye and go,' said Dick in a calm voice. 'I've told you that Ned and Pongo are staying with us for the now.'

'Where *is* Ned?' demanded Tiger Dan, looking as if he would burst with rage at any moment. 'Wait till I get my hands on him. Wait . . .'

He began to walk towards the caravans – but Pongo was not having any of that! He leapt straight off the roof of the caravan on to the horrified man.

Go to **177**.

183

'George and I will get you something to eat,' said Anne. 'We called at the farm on the way back and got lots more delicious food from Mrs Mackie. She gave me a huge bar of chocolate, too. Wasn't it kind of her?'

In no time at all George and Anne had got a large meal ready, and they ate it sitting on the rocky ledge. Pongo sat with them, eating some bananas that Anne had bought in the town specially for him. He threw the skins on the ground when he had finished with them, but Ned spoke to him sternly, and made him pick the skins up and put them with the rest of the rubbish.

'No sign of Tiger Dan and Lou,' said Julian. 'With a bit of luck they're miles away by now.'

Go to **185**.

184

They decided to push the caravan up the slope towards the sharp drop.

'Don't let it go too far,' warned Julian, 'or we'll lose it over the edge.'

When they were clear of the hole, they stopped pushing and turned their attention to the planks of wood. Too late, they realised that the caravan was very slowly rolling back towards them.

'Quick!' shouted Julian. 'Stop it before it breaks the planks and slides into the hole, otherwise we'll never get it out!'

As he spoke, the caravan gave a lurch, and one wheel slid to the edge of the hole.

Go to **187**.

185

If you have arrived from **183**, *score* ○ ○.

'Let's go and explore!' said George eagerly. 'I'm longing to go down the hole and Make Discoveries!'

'I think it would be a good idea to take some food down into the hill with us,' said Julian. 'We may be down there for ages, and we don't want to have to come back at tea-time.'

They packed up some bread, butter and ham, a cake and a large bar of chocolate. Anne remembered a knife, too. At last they were ready.

Go to **179**.

If you have arrived from **174**, *score* ⌒⌒⌒.

'It really doesn't need all of us to go into town and buy torches,' said Dick. 'I'll stay here and keep Ned and Pongo company. Don't forget to post that letter to Mum and Dad, Julian.'

They had written a long letter to their parents, telling them of all the exciting things that had happened. Julian put the letter into his pocket.

'I'll post it all right,' he said. 'Well, I suppose we'd better go now. Come on, girls. Keep a look out, Dick, in case those rogues come back.'

George, Timmy, Anne and Julian went down the hill together, Timmy running on in front. Pongo climbed on to the roof of the red caravan to watch them go. Ned and Dick sat down in the warm sun on the ledge.

'It's nice up here,' said Ned, 'much nicer than down below. I wonder where everyone thinks Pongo and I have gone. I bet Mr Giorgio, who owns the circus, is angry that the chimpanzee's gone. I bet he sends someone up to fetch us.'

Go to **182**.

187

They all made frantic attempts to keep the caravan out of the hole, but it was no use. They felt the caravan slipping further and further away from their hands. Finally it stopped, with one wheel stuck firmly in the hole!

'Oh, no!' said George. 'Now what are we going to do?'

Anne had turned pale. 'Supposing the caravan falls down into the hole?' she said. 'We'd never be able to get it out.'

'There's no need to worry about it falling right in, Anne,' said Julian in a comforting voice. 'The caravan is far wider than the hole. But there's no doubt that getting it back on to firm ground is going to be a real problem.'

The best way of straightening the caravan seemed to be by pushing from the side that was tilted into the hole, but when they started to shove from that side the caravan wouldn't budge!

For the next half an hour they pulled and pushed and shoved and hauled, but the caravan stayed firmly stuck.

'It's no good,' said Julian at last, 'we'll have to think of some other way of getting it out of there!'

Go to **192**.

188

'Why shouldn't I go first?' said George furiously. 'Just because you're a boy doesn't mean you should always be the first one to explore things. I'm not scared of anything – and I'm going first!'

George looked so fierce that Julian laughed.

'All right,' he said. 'You go first. But be careful, won't you?'

'Of course I will,' said George scornfully. She really hated being treated like a girl in any way!

'What are you going to do with your torch, George?' asked Ned. 'You won't be able to hold it in your hand climbing up there, will you?'

'I'll hold it between my teeth,' said George, but when she tried to put her torch in her mouth, she found it was impossible. The torch was much too big and heavy. She could only just get her jaws round it.

'Oh, darn!' she said. 'I'll have to stick it in the back pocket of my jeans and hope it doesn't fall out.'

'If we all shine our torches upwards, that should give you enough light to climb up,' said Dick. 'Off you go!'

Go to **196**.

Timmy sat quietly at George's feet while she and Dick pondered the problem.

'If one of us leant out of the hole, and the other one lifted Timmy up, do you think we could manage like that?' said George at last.

Dick looked doubtful. 'I suppose we could try it,' he said, 'but Timmy's very heavy, and he won't like being lifted up – he'll probably squirm a lot. I don't think it would work, George.'

'No, I think you're right,' said George. 'Perhaps we'd better call the others and see if they can come up with a good idea.'

'Julian! Ned! Anne!' shouted Dick.

Three heads appeared in the hole.

'What's the trouble?' Julian called.

'We can't think of a way to get Timmy up there,' George said. 'Have any of you got any ideas?'

'Hold on,' said Julian. 'I think we'd better come down. We can't talk to you like this.'

The three of them climbed back down again, and

then they all sat down on the floor, trying to think of a solution.

'I've got an idea,' said Ned at last. 'If I stand on Julian's shoulders, maybe one of you could lift Timmy up to me, and I could lift him to someone leaning down from the hole.'

'The only thing I can think of,' said George, 'is for one of us to go back to the caravans and get my sleeping bag. We could haul him up in that.'

If you think they should try Ned's idea, go to **194**.
If you think they should try George's idea, go to **200**.

190

'But the coast *is* clear,' said Julian. 'I told you, Dan and Lou have gone off somewhere on the bus. We saw them!'

'Yes,' answered Dick, 'but how do you know that they're going to be away overnight? Perhaps they've done what we did. Perhaps they got off at the first stop like Julian did, and they're coming up here to see if we've left the caravans unguarded.'

'I'll tell you what,' said Anne. 'We could wait for a little while, so that if they *do* come back they'll see we're still here.'

'And while we're waiting, we could have something to eat,' added Dick. 'It's long past our lunch time, and I'm starving.'

Go to **183**.

191

They decided to move the caravan backwards towards the trees.

'Don't push too hard,' warned Julian. 'We don't want it to run away down the hill.'

They all put their shoulders against the caravan.

'Ready?' said George. 'One, two, three – heave!'

Slowly and heavily the caravan moved back until it was clear of the hole.

'Now for some exploring!' said George excitedly.

Go to **203**.

192

By now they were all hot and thirsty.

'I've got a good idea,' said Anne. 'I'll go and get us all some nice cold lemonade, and we can sit and drink it while we think about what to do.'

The others all thought a drink would be marvellous, so Anne disappeared into the other caravan, and soon came back with several big glasses. The children flopped on the ground, drinking thirstily.

'Well,' said Dick at last, 'how are we going to get the caravan straight again?'

'We really need something strong to pull it out,' said George, almost to herself.

'What about the horses?' suggested Anne. 'What

about Dobby and Trotter? One of them could pull it out, couldn't they?'

'I KNOW!' shouted Ned suddenly, so loudly that they all jumped. 'What about Old Lady? She could pull it out! What about the elephant, then?'

If you think they should use one of the horses, go to **197**.
If you think they should try the elephant, go to **202**.

193

The children had all put on extra jumpers, because they thought it might be cold inside the hill. Ned had been lent an old one of Dick's. They were glad of them as soon as they started to walk down the dark passage that led to the first cave, for the air was very chilly.

They came to the small cave, and Julian flashed his torch to show them where the footholds went up the wall to a hole in the roof.

'It's very exciting,' said George, thrilled. 'I like

this sort of thing. Where does that hole in the roof lead to, I wonder? Let's go up and have a look. I'll go first, Julian.'

'No, you won't,' said her cousin firmly. 'I'm going first. You don't know what might be at the top!'

If you think George should go first, go to **188**.
If you think Julian should, go to **198**.

194

'Are you sure you can hold Timmy?' asked Julian. 'He's very heavy, you know, Ned.'

'Well, I'm used to moving the seats from the Big Top, and carrying props around,' said Ned. 'There's a lot of hard work involved in running a circus, you know. I'm quite strong, even though I ain't tall for my age.'

'Let's try it, shall we?' said George. 'If we stay here discussing it for much longer, it will be too late to explore the rest of the caves. I haven't been up into that big cave yet!'

They all scrambled to their feet. Dick climbed swiftly up into the big cavern, and then lay down on his stomach, with his head and shoulders sticking out of the entrance hole. Julian bent down, and Ned scrambled nimbly up on to his shoulders. Then Julian braced himself against the wall, and between them Anne and George picked up Timmy and gave him to Ned. Ned was surprised to find just how heavy Timmy was, but he managed to get a reasonably firm grip on the big dog, and he slowly straightened up. Timmy, though very puzzled by it all, lay perfectly still in Ned's arms.

Go to **206**.

'You two boys can ride up the hill on Old Lady's back if you like,' said Larry, as he untied Old Lady's chain.

'That would be brilliant!' said Julian. 'How do we get up on her back, Larry?'

Larry winked at Ned. 'Up! Up!' he said to Old Lady. Old Lady curled her trunk round Julian's waist and lifted him off the ground and on to her back! Then she lifted Ned up, and they set off up the hill to the caravans.

Julian found riding on an elephant very interesting. It was rather like being in a boat on a choppy sea, and she took such big strides that it was not long before they were back at the camp site. The others were amazed to see Julian and Ned riding on the elephant, and Timmy didn't know what to make of it at all!

Larry had brought Old Lady's harness with him, and soon they had it attached to the front of the caravan. Larry guided Old Lady forward while

Julian, Dick and Ned supported the caravan in case it tilted the wrong way. With two strong pulls Old Lady had it safely on firm ground again.

'Oh, thank you, Larry!' exclaimed Anne. 'Thank you too, Old Lady! You are clever!'

'Well, I must be getting back,' said Larry. 'Don't you worry. Ned. I won't tell no one that I know where you are, promise!'

'Thanks, Larry,' said Ned. 'You're a real pal.'

'And now,' said Julian, as the elephant trundled away, 'to get down that hole and start exploring!'

Go to **203**.

196

George started to climb. The footholds were strong nails, driven into the rock of the cave wall, and made climbing fairly easy. Timmy stood on the ground, gazing up at George with an expression on his face that seemed to say, 'What is she up to now?'

George had climbed about halfway up when she suddenly seemed to slip. At the same time there was a clinking noise, and something came tumbling down on to the floor of the cave. It was followed immediately by another clinking noise, and then George slid down the wall and landed in a heap on the floor!

'George!' shouted Anne in alarm. 'George, are you all right?'

There was no answer. George didn't move. The others looked at each other in horror.

'Oh, help,' said Dick. 'I think she might have been knocked out!'

Go to **201**.

'I don't think we've got enough time to go down and see if Old Lady can help us,' said Julian, 'but we could certainly try one of the horses. George, would you and Dick like to go over to the field and get one of them? I'll stay here with Ned and Anne and keep an eye on the caravan, just in case it tips any more.'

George and Dick set off for the nearby field where Dobby and Trotter were kept.

'We'd better try Dobby, I think,' puffed George as they ran. 'He's a bit stronger than Trotter.'

Dobby and Trotter came to meet them as they crossed the field. The children had been to see them every day, to make sure they were all right, and to take them carrots and apples. Dobby was obviously not very pleased about being taken out of the field without a treat of some sort, but George and Dick had no trouble leading him back to the camp site.

George swiftly harnessed Dobby to the caravan.

'It's lucky we can still get at the driver's end of the van,' she said, as she buckled on the reins. 'Otherwise we'd be in real trouble!'

Anne thought to herself that they were in quite enough trouble as it was, but she said nothing.

Go to **205**.

198

If you have arrived from **204**, *score* ◁ ◁ ◁ ◁.

Julian put his torch in his back pocket, as he needed both hands to climb with. It wasn't difficult, though he was careful to test each of the footholds before putting his weight on them, in case any of them were not firm.

He got to the hole in the roof and popped his head through. Then he gave a cry of astonishment.

You won't believe it! There's a most ENORMOUS cavern here – almost as big as a football pitch – and the walls are all glittering with something – phosphorescence, I should think.'

He scrambled out of the hole and stood on the floor of the immense cave. Its walls twinkled with their strange light. Julian turned off his torch, and found there was almost enough phosphorescent light in the cave to see by! He stuck his head down the hole and called to the others.

'Come on, all of you!'

Anne and Ned scrambled up without any trouble, but back in the small cave Dick and George were struck by the same thought.

'How on *earth* are we going to get Timmy up there?' said George.

Go to **189**.

199

The five children explored every nook and cranny of the gleaming cave, but there was no sign of any stolen goods. They were all rather surprised not to find anything, as the great cavern seemed an ideal place to store things. It was dry and cool, with a smooth floor.

'Do you think there are any tunnels leading off this cave?' asked Dick when they sat down for a rest.

'I think there must be,' said Julian. 'After all, we're pretty certain that they're hiding *something*, and not just exploring the caves for fun! They wouldn't have made such a fuss about us camping if they

hadn't got something to conceal.'

'I think we ought to explore carefully all round the edge of the cave,' said George. 'It's so big that if we just stand in the middle and flash our torches round the walls we might easily miss something.'

'Good idea,' said Julian. 'We'd better split up – it'll be quicker. Ned, you come with me and Anne. George, Dick and Timmy can go the other way. Shout when you discover something.'

If you want to go with Julian, go to **213**.
If you want to go with George, go to **218**.

200

'I think your idea is a bit too risky, Ned,' said Julian. 'It would be too easy for you to get hurt, and we certainly don't want that!'

'I'll go back and get the sleeping bag,' said Dick. 'It won't take long.'

He dashed off, and while the others waited, Ned

told them some more about life with the circus. It was very interesting – all about how the Big Top was put up and taken down, with everyone who worked for the circus taking part.

'Even the little kids collect the cushions off the seats,' he finished, as Dick came panting back.

Ned and Anne climbed back up to the big cave, while George and Dick unzipped the sleeping bag and lifted Timmy into the foot of it. He looked at them as if he thought they were mad!

When he was safely zipped inside, Julian took hold of the open end and began to climb up to the cavern. George and Dick supported Timmy's weight from below until Anne and Ned were able to help Julian pull the sleeping bag up through the hole. Poor Timmy really hated being hauled about like a sack of potatoes, but he put up with it patiently, and enjoyed the fuss that was made of him when he eventually emerged from the sleeping bag, looking somewhat surprised.

Go to **210**.

Julian bent over George, shining his torch on her face. Her eyes were closed, but he could see that she was breathing.

'Well, she hasn't killed herself, anyway!' he said, sounding more cheerful than he felt.

'Of course I haven't killed myself,' said a cross voice. 'I'm tougher than that!'

George sat up and glared round at the circle of anxious faces. She looked a bit pale and shaken, and there was a bump on her forehead, but otherwise she was all right.

'What happened?' asked Julian, as George stretched her arms and legs cautiously.

'A couple of nails fell out of the wall,' she answered. 'Didn't you hear them hit the floor of the cave?'

'Is that what we heard. I wondered what it was,' said Anne.

'They should be on the ground somewhere,' said Julian. 'We'll have to find them and stick them back in the wall, otherwise we won't be able to climb up. Come on, we'd better have a look. George, you sit still for a moment and get your breath back.'

George nodded. She really did feel rather sick, and was glad to sit quietly while the others searched. They all shone their torches on the ground, and before long sharp-eyed Anne pounced on something shiny.

'Here's one of them,' she said.

'And here's the other,' said Dick, a moment or two later.

'Come on,' said Julian. 'We must stick them back in the wall.'

Go to **204**.

202

'Ned!' chorused the rest of them. 'What a brilliant idea!'

'An elephant can pull the most enormous weights,' Ned went on. 'Used for all sorts of things, elephants are. She'll be able to pull that caravan out in no time. Come on, let's go down and get her!'

'Hang on a moment, Ned,' said Julian. 'Do you think the man who looks after her will mind? Won't he be afraid that Dan and Lou would hear that he had helped us, and try and get even with him?'

'Not likely,' said Ned. 'Larry ain't afraid of Dan and Lou. He's got Old Lady to protect him. Not even Dan and Lou would mess about with Old Lady – she can be real fierce when she wants to be!'

'How will she get up here, though?' asked George. 'The path is quite steep in places.'

'Don't you know nothing about elephants, George?' asked Ned. 'An elephant can walk over almost any kind of hill or mountain – marvellous, they are. Old Lady won't have any trouble getting up here, you wait and see!'

'Well, I think it's a brilliant idea of yours, Ned,'

said Julian. 'Come on, then, let's go down to the circus and see Larry.'

Go to **207**.

203

If you have arrived from **205**, *score* ᗒ ᗒ ᗒ ᗒ.
If you have arrived from **195**, *score* ᗒ ᗒ ᗒ ᗒ ᗒ.

They pulled all the planks away from the hole and piled them on one side. As soon as Pongo saw the hole he drew back in fear.

'He's remembered the darkness down there,' said George. 'He doesn't like it. Come on, Pongo. You'll be all right. We've all got torches. Look!'

She turned her torch on and shone it down the hole, lighting it up, but nothing would persuade Pongo to go down that hole again. He cried like a baby when Ned tried to make him.

'It's no good,' said Julian. 'You'll have to stay up here with him, Ned.'

'Not likely!' said Ned. 'I'll miss all the excitement. We can tie old Pongo up to a wheel of the van so that he won't wander off.'

So Pongo was tied firmly to one of the caravan wheels.

'You stay here until we come back,' said Ned, putting a pail of water beside him in case he should want a drink.

Pongo was sad to see them go, but nothing would have made him go down that hole again! So he sat watching the children disappear one by one. Timmy jumped down, too, and then they were all gone. What would happen now?

Go to **193**.

251

'That's going to be difficult,' said Dick. 'Nobody could stand on the footholds and hammer nails back into the wall at the same time, that's certain. Has anyone got any ideas?'

'I know,' said Ned. 'I can stand on Julian's shoulders – I'll be able to reach the place where George fell off like that. I'm used to riding horses bareback – doing somersaults and standing on me hands, and things like that – so I shouldn't have any trouble standing on Julian's shoulders,'

'Good idea, Ned,' said Julian approvingly. 'You can use the base of my torch for a hammer. Quick, give Ned the nails.'

Ned put the nails into one of his pockets. Julian crouched against the wall, and Ned sprang swiftly and easily on to his shoulders. He soon found the right places for the two nails, and hammered them home firmly. Then he jumped down again.

'All done,' he said.

'Well done, Ned, it was fantastic the way you got up on Julian's shoulders like that. You are clever,' said Anne admiringly.

'Thanks,' mumbled Ned, feeling very pleased.

'Right,' said Julian. 'This time I'm going up first.'

Go to **198**.

205

George pulled the long reins forward over Dobby's head, and stepped back.

'Mind you don't fall over the edge, George,' cautioned Julian.

'You and Dick steady the caravan, Julian,' she said, 'and I'll guide Dobby. Come on, Dobby. Come on now.'

Dobby moved forward, and the harness tautened. George moved slowly backwards, encouraging Dobby all the time, and slowly but surely the caravan moved forward and up out of the hole.

Soon the caravan was standing with both its wheels on firm ground.

'Well done, Dobby,' said George, giving him a pat. 'Well done!' She offered him an apple, which he ate with loud, crunching noises.

'Right,' said Julian. 'You take Dobby back to his field, George, and I'll just check that the caravan's OK.'

It didn't take long to get Dobby back in the field, and George raced back to join the others.

'Now to go exploring at last!' said Dick, his eyes shining.

Go to **203**.

206

George and Anne watched anxiously as Ned slowly, slowly stood up straight. He was able to lean against the wall of the cave, which helped a bit.

When he was finally standing upright, he looked up at Dick.

'If you're ready, Dick, I'll try and lift Timmy up to you,' he said.

'Ned, hang on, I've got an idea!' called George. 'If Dick moves back so that only his head shows in the hole, and he calls Timmy, Timmy should jump up to him. Try it, and see what happens.'

'OK, George,' Ned replied. 'Brace yourself, Julian! Right, Dick, whenever you're ready!'

'Timmy! Timmy!' called Dick. 'Come on, boy!'

Timmy looked up at Dick, who called him again. Ned felt the dog's muscles tense, and then Timmy had sprung upwards out of his arms. For a horrifying moment it looked as if he wouldn't make it, but Dick managed to grab his front paws and pulled him into the cave.

'Phew!' said George. 'I'm glad that's over.'

Go to **210**.

Ned and Julian set off down the hill. Pongo wanted to go too, but Ned thought it would be easier if he stayed behind, so Anne gave him a couple more bananas.

'We'll need some rope or harness or something,' said Julian as they ran. 'To attach Old Lady to the caravan, I mean.'

'You don't have to worry about that,' replied Ned. 'We've got a special harness for her. Old Lady pulls a caravan when we're on the move.'

'Oh, yes,' said Julian. 'I remember. She was pulling the caravan at the front of the procession when you came past our house.'

By now the two boys had reached the circus camp, and Ned ran straight to Larry's caravan. Larry was sitting on the steps, holding a cup of tea and enjoying the sunshine.

'Larry, can you and Old Lady help my friends, please?' said Ned.

'Where have you been, young Ned?' asked Larry.

'Mr Giorgio's wild about that chimp disappearing, let me tell you.'

'I know,' said Ned, 'but I'll explain about that later. We need Old Lady, Larry. *Please* help us.'

''Course I'll help you,' said Larry with a smile. 'What do you want me to do?'

Julian and Ned explained rapidly what had happened to the caravan.

'Old Lady won't have any trouble pulling the caravan out,' said Larry. 'She'll enjoy it. Come on, let's go and get her.'

Go to **195**.

208

When Julian and George reached the end of the tunnel they found that it ended in a rocky wall. The light came from a small slit in the rock, through which they could see the sky and the tops of some trees.

'This must have been where an underground stream reached the surface,' said Julian. 'Well, it's nice to see the sky and breathe some fresh air, but I think we'd better get back to the others.'

They had to crawl right out of the hole to turn round, and once again, Julian led the way. After a few minutes Julian stopped.

'George!' he called. 'The tunnel divides, and I've no idea at all which way we came out!'

George groaned. 'Well, we'll just have to try one way and hope for the best. We can always come back. Which fork shall we try?'

If you think they should take the right-hand fork, go to **221**.

If you think they should take the left-hand fork, go to **216**.

There were muffled scufflings, and one or two groans, and then Julian gave a shout.

'That's it, George, I've come unstuck. Thanks!'

George let go of Julian's legs and rubbed her aching arms. There was no room to turn round in the tunnel, so they would have to wriggle backwards to the place were the two passages joined. Timmy decided he was going to turn round, so George had to wait while he squirmed and scuffled. She was afraid that he wouldn't be able to manage in such a small space, but at last he got himself round the right away.

George found that her elbows and knees were getting very sore, and she was glad when they got back to the place where the passage divided.

'Now, we go down that one,' said George, pointing to the mouth of the left hand tunnel, 'don't we?'

Go to **216**.

210

If you have arrived from **206**, *score* ◯◁.

When everyone had climbed up into the huge cavern, they began exploring.

'It's like Aladdin's cave!' said Anne. 'Isn't that a strange light shining from the walls and the roof, Julian?'

'What an enormous place!' said Dick. 'Do you suppose this is where the men hide their stuff, whatever it is?'

Julian turned on his torch and swung it round the cavern, picking out the dark, rocky corners.

'Can't see anything hidden,' he said, 'but we'd better explore the cave properly before we go on.'

Go to **199**.

The other three came across the cave in a rush.

'What have you found?' asked Ned breathlessly.

Dick flashed his torch on to the narrow opening.

'There seems to be a tunnel down here,' he said. 'Shall we explore it?'

'Of course,' answered Julian. 'Now, I'll go first, then George. I think it would be a good idea if the rest of you stayed here, just in case anything happens.'

Neither Dick nor Ned was very pleased at having to stay behind, but they could see the sense of what Julian said. Anne was rather glad that she didn't have to wriggle into the dark little tunnel!

Julian and George dropped down on their knees and disappeared into the entrance. Timmy followed George, of course, and Ned, Dick and Anne sat down to wait for the others to come back.

Julian and George wriggled along on their stomachs. Fortunately the floor of the passage was as smooth and dry as the rest of the cave. It was terribly dark – there was no phosphorescence on the walls, and of course no light from outside could reach it. They had to hold their torches in front of them as they moved.

It seemed to George that they had been wriggling along the tunnel for a very long time when suddenly Julian stopped.

'What is it, Ju?' asked George. 'Have you found something?'

'No,' said Julian, 'but I think I can smell fresh air. Turn off your torch a moment, George. I want to see if there's any light coming into the tunnel from outside.'

They both turned their torches off, and for a moment the darkness seemed thick and black. However, as their eyes grew used to it, they could see a faint grey light ahead of them.

'I think that must be daylight,' said Julian. 'I'll bet this tunnel opens out on to the surface! Come on.'

They turned on their torches and moved

forward again. Sure enough, they had only gone a few more metres when the light became brighter and brighter.

Go to **208**.

212

'Look here!' said George suddenly, and she pulled some leather boxes out of a bag. 'Jewellery!'

She opened the boxes. The children exclaimed in awe. Diamonds flashed brilliantly, rubies glowed, emeralds shone green. Necklaces, bracelets, brooches, rings – the beautiful things gleamed in the light of the five torches. There was a tiara in one box that seemed to be made only of big diamonds. Anne picked it out of its box gently, and put it on her hair.

'I feel like a princess!' she exclaimed.

'You look like one, too,' said Ned, gazing at her in

admiration. 'Why don't you try some of the other things on?'

Anne put on necklaces, bracelets and rings, and sat there on the rocky ledge covered with diamonds, and looking like a princess. Then she took them off and put them back carefully into their satin-lined boxes.

'Well – what a haul those two villains have made!' exclaimed Julian, pulling some gleaming silver plate out of a sack. 'They must be very clever burglars.'

Go to **220**.

213

If you have arrived from **216***, score* ◐ ◐ ◐ ◐.

Julian, Ned and Anne made their way slowly along the wall of the cavern, flashing their torches around the gleaming walls and along the floor. Julian gave a sudden exclamation and picked something up from the floor.

'A spent match!' he said. 'That shows that Lou and Dan have been here. Come on, let's see if we can find the way out of this cave.'

Right at the far end, halfway up the gleaming wall, was a large hole, rather like a tunnel. Julian called the others over to have look.

'This must be the way they went,' he said, climbing up to it and shining his torch inside. 'They dropped an empty box of matches just here.'

It was a curious tunnel, no higher than their shoulders in some places, and it wound about as it went further into the hill. Julian was sure that at one time a stream had flowed through it.

Go to **223**.

If you have arrived from **219**, *score* ◯⌐.

'I think we should go and tell the police,' repeated Anne. 'We could show them where the stolen goods are, and they could lie in wait for Dan and Lou when they come back to collect them.'

Julian looked thoughtful.

'That's a good idea,' he said. 'The police would catch those two villains red-handed, and that would be the end of their careers in crime!'

'Who's going to go to the police station, and who's going to stay here?' asked George, secretly hoping that she would be able to stay in the cave. She wanted to see Dan and Lou's faces when the police cornered them.

'I'd better go to the police station, and I think Anne should come with me,' answered Julian. 'You three stay here, and if Dan and Lou turn up before we get back, you three will have to stop them leaving the caves.'

'How are we going to do that?' asked Ned.

'I'm sure we'll be able to think of something!' said Dick with a laugh. 'We've dealt with some nasty villains before now.'

Go to **222**.

215

'Can't see any daylight shining down the hole,' said Julian, puzzled.

He came up against a blank wall, and was surprised. Where was the hole? Had they missed their way? Then he flashed his torch above him and saw the hole there, but there was no daylight.

'Oh no!' exclaimed Julian in horror. 'What do you think's happened?'

'What?' asked everyone in panic.

'The hole is closed!' said Julian. 'We can't get out! Somebody's been along and put the planks back.' He pushed at one of the planks. It moved just a little, then hit something solid. 'I think they've moved the caravan back over the hole,' he said. 'We can't get out!'

They all stared up at the closed entrance in dismay. They were prisoners!

'What are we going to do?' said George. 'Julian – what *are* we going to do?'

Go to **224**.

216

If you have arrived from **209**, *score* ◁ ◁.

'That's the one,' said Julian, and they set off down the left-hand fork. Timmy scuffled along behind George. He was thoroughly fed up with the tunnel. He had to crouch down all the time, and it wasn't at all comfortable! Luckily for Timmy, they only had to wriggle a little bit further before they found themselves back in the big cave.

'Well?' said the other three together. 'Did you find anything exciting?'

Julian shook his head. 'No,' he replied. 'The tunnel opens out on to the hillside. – I think a stream used to run through it. There was nothing hidden there.'

He got to his feet. 'George, you and Dick go on searching this side of the cave. The rest of us will go back and search the other side.'

'Right,' said Dick, and off they went.

Go to **213**.

217

If you have arrived from **228**, *score* ⌁.

Ned put down his torch and undid a sack. He slid in his hand – and brought out a piece of shining gold plate!

'Look!' said Ned. 'So that's what the police were after last year when they came and searched the camp! And it was safely hidden here. Look at all these things. They must have robbed the Queen herself!'

The sack was full of exquisite pieces of gold plate – cups, dishes, small trays. The children set them all out on the ledge. How they gleamed in the light of their torches!

'They're thieves in a very big way,' said Julian. 'No

doubt about that. Let's look in this box.'

The box was not locked, and the lid opened easily. Inside was a piece of china, so fragile that it looked as if it might break at a breath!

'Well, I don't know anything about china,' said Julian, 'but I suppose this is a very precious piece, worth thousands of pounds. A collector of china would probably give a very large sum for it. What rogues Dan and Lou are!'

Go to **212**.

218

George, Dick and Timmy set off, sticking close to the edge and sweeping their torches up to the roof and then down to the ground.

'The walls really are incredibly smooth,' said Dick. 'I think this used to be an underground lake, and the water wore the walls away over thousands of years.'

George gave a shiver. She had a vision of the cave suddenly filling with water and drowning them all, and for a moment felt rather scared. Then she gave herself a shake and told herself to stop being so silly. No water had flowed through this cave for years – it was much too cold and dry.

'Look, George,' called Dick, who was a little way in front of her. 'This looks like the entrance to a tunnel!'

They could see an opening in the cave wall. It was only a small opening – so low that they would have to crawl into it on hands and knees, but it was definitely worth exploring.

'I'll call the others!' said George. 'Julian, Ned, Anne!'

'Anne–Anne–Anne!' Her voice echoed in the great cave.

Go to **211**.

'What good would hiding the treasure do?' asked George. 'Dan and Lou will both get into a terrible rage and start looking for it.'

'Yes, exactly,' said Dick, 'and while they're looking for it, we can trap them in the tunnel, and then go and get the police.'

'We don't need to hide the treasure,' argued George. 'All we have to do is hide near the caravans, wait until they come along and enter the tunnel, then we'll have trapped them anyway!'

'They may have another way out of the tunnel that we haven't found,' retorted Dick.

'I don't think there can be any other entrance, or if there is they don't know about it,' said Anne thoughtfully. 'After all, if they could have got into the tunnels any other way, they wouldn't have tried so hard to make us move, would they?'

'You're right, Anne,' admitted Dick. 'Well, what shall we do now?'

Go to **214**.

220

'I bet I can guess how they work,' said Dick. 'Lou's a wonderful acrobat, isn't he? I bet he does all the climbing up walls and over roofs and into windows – and Tiger Dan stands below and catches everything he throws down.'

'You're about right,' said Ned, handling a beautiful silver cup. 'Lou could climb anywhere – up ivy, up pipes – even up the bare wall of a house, I shouldn't wonder. And jump! He can jump like a cat. He and Tiger Dan have been in this business a long time, I expect. That's where Uncle Dan went at night, of course, when we were on tour, and I woke up and found him gone out of the caravan.'

'And I guess he stores the stolen goods in that wagon of his you showed us,' said Julian, remembering. 'You told us how angry he was with you once when you went and rummaged about in it. He probably stored them there, and then he and Lou came up here each year and hid the stuff underground – waiting until the police had given up the search for the stolen things – and then they can come and get it and sell it somewhere safe.'

'A very clever plan,' said Dick. 'What a fine chance they've got – wandering about from place to place like that, hearing of jewels or plate – slipping out at night – and Lou climbing into bedrooms like a cat. I wonder how they found this place – it makes a brilliant hiding place!'

'Yes, nobody would ever dream it was here!' said George.

'And then we go and put our caravan bang on top of the entrance – just when they want to put something in and take something out!' said Julian. 'We *must* have annoyed them!'

Go to **225**.

'The right-hand fork, I think,' said Julian. 'How's Timmy? Is he managing to keep up with us?'

'Oh, yes,' said George. 'He's fine.'

They moved forward along the tunnel, but they had not gone very far before the floor of the tunnel started to slope upwards. George was sure that the tunnel they had come down from the cavern had been more or less flat. She was sure they had chosen the wrong fork. She opened her mouth to call to Julian that they had made a mistake, when she heard him shout something.

'Oh, no!'

'What's the matter, Julian?' George called back.

'I'm stuck!' he said. 'The tunnel gets much narrower here, and I've got my head and shoulders wedged.'

George shone her torch forward, and, sure enough, there were Julian's legs, squirming around as he tried to free himself. It looked so funny that George started to laugh.

'All right,' came Julian's voice, sounding rather muffled. 'I'm sure I do look funny, but you'll have to help me, George. Can you pull on my legs?'

'I'll try,' said George, doubtfully. She put down her torch and grabbed hold of Julian's feet. She told Timmy to move back, and then she started to wriggle backwards on her stomach, pulling Julian's feet as she went.

Go to **209**.

222

Julian and Anne made their way back along the passage and down into the big cavern. They crossed the cavern and climbed through the hole and down into the passage that led back to the entrance. Anne was very pleased to see the daylight pouring into the dark tunnel. The fresh air smelled wonderful as they clambered up on to the heather.

The camp site looked peaceful, just as they had

left it. Pongo was sitting beside one of the caravans, obviously fed up. He was overjoyed to see Julian and Anne, and jumped to his feet, dancing up and down and chattering excitedly.

'I'll just get him a banana, Julian,' said Anne.

'We haven't got time to waste over things like that,' said Julian impatiently. 'You can give Pongo a banana when we come back with the police. Now come on!'

'Oh, poor Pongo,' said Anne, but Julian had already set off down the track that led to the road, and didn't hear her.

Left on his own once again, Pongo sat down, looking very sulky. He started to rock backwards and forwards, holding his feet with his paws, grumbling to himself. As he rocked, he pulled the rope that tied him to the caravan, and little by little the knot began to work loose. He stopped rocking after a while, and leaned over to have a drink from the bucket of water that had been left for him. As he did so, the end of the rope fell away from the caravan, and Pongo found he was free!

Jumping to his feet, he set off down the hill after Julian and Anne.

Go to **227**.

223

The others followed Julian into the tunnel, which went on for some way. Soon Anne was beginning to feel it must go on for ever. In spite of their torches she was rather scared. No light from outside could ever reach these passages, and it would be terrifying to be lost in them without a light of any sort.

At last they came to a place where the wall at one side widened out and made a rocky shelf. Julian, who was in the lead as usual, flashed his torch on to it.

'Look!' he shouted. 'I think we might have found the place where those thieves keep the stolen goods. Look at all this!'

The others crowded up as closely as they could,

shining their torches. On the wide, rocky shelf were piled all sorts of boxes, sacks and packages. The children stared at them.

'What's in them?' said Ned, full of intense curiosity. 'I bet it's stuff they've stolen!'

'It might be something else,' argued Dick. 'Supplies of food, or something like that, in case they ever have to hide out in these caves and tunnels.'

If you think Ned is right, go to **217**.
If you think Dick is right, go to **228**.

224

The five children stared at each other in dismay. Julian didn't answer George. He was angry with himself for not thinking that this might happen. Although Dan and Lou had been seen getting on the bus with bags, they might easily not have been spending the night away – the bags might have contained things they wanted to sell – stolen goods of some kind.

'They came back quickly – and came up the hill, I suppose, to have another try at getting Ned and Pongo to come back,' said Julian. 'Well, now we'll all have to think really hard about what we're going to do. Has anyone got any ideas?'

'We could try and shift the caravan, I suppose,' said Dick doubtfully.

'Or we could try and find another way out of the cave,' suggested Anne unexpectedly.

If you think they should try and move the caravan, go to **232**.
If you think they should try and find another way out of the cave, go to **237**.

225

'What are we going to do about it?' said Dick.

'Tell the police, of course,' said Julian promptly.

'What do you think? I'd like to see the face of the policeman who first sees this little haul.'

They replaced all the beautiful, gleaming things in the boxes and sacks, then sat down to discuss what they were going to do next.

'I think we should go back and get the police,' said Anne, who would have felt much safer with one or two large constables around.

'I vote we go on and explore the rest of the tunnels first,' said Julian.

'No,' said Dick, 'we ought to hide this stuff so that if Dan and Lou come looking for it, they won't be able to find it.'

If you agree with Anne, go to **214**.
If you agree with Julian, go to **230**.
If you agree with Dick, go to **219**.

'Maybe at one time it ran across this cave and down the tunnel we came up by,' said Julian. 'Yes, look – there's a big groove in the floor of the cave here – the stream must have run there once, and then for some reason it went a different way.'

'Let's get back,' said Ned. 'I want to know if Pongo's all right. I don't feel very comfortable about him. I'm cold, too. Let's go back to the sunshine and have something to eat. I don't want a picnic down here after all.'

'Good idea,' said the others, and they made their way back through the tunnel. They passed the rock shelf on which lay the treasure, and came at last to the enormous gleaming cavern. Down they went, Julian and George trying to manage Timmy between them, but it was very awkward with such a big dog.

Finally they made their way along the passage to the entrance hole. They all felt quite pleased at the idea of going up into the sunshine again.

Go to **215**.

227

Julian was walking so fast that Anne had trouble keeping up with him. He wanted to get down to the road and get the bus to the nearest village, where he could contact the police. Anne puffed along behind him, wondering whether it would perhaps have been easier if she had stayed with the other three.

'Julian!' she called. 'Julian, wait for me!'

Julian turned round to look at her, and as he did so, he saw Pongo, running down the hill after them. He shouted a warning to Anne, but it was too late. Pongo jumped on her from behind and knocked her flat!

Anne fell down in a heap with Pongo on top of her. Julian came racing up and pulled Pongo off his sister, then helped Anne to her feet.

'Are you all right?' he asked anxiously.

Anne gave a rather wobbly laugh.

'Yes,' she said. 'I'm just a bit shaken, that's all. Oh, Pongo, you did give me a fright!'

'We'd better take him back and tie him up again,' said Julian. 'Come on.'

They led Pongo back to the caravans, and Julian tied him up with the tightest knots he could make. Anne gave Pongo a banana, and checked that his water bucket was full. The two of them were just about to set off down the hill again when they heard the sound of voices.

'Quick!' said Julian, 'back into the tunnel. That might be Dan and Lou!'

They scrambled back into the tunnel as fast as they could, then they set off back to where the others were waiting.

Go to **233**.

'Let's have a look,' said Julian, opening one of the boxes. He shone his torch inside it.

'What is it, Julian?' said George excitedly. 'Is it stolen goods?'

Julian shook his head. 'No, you were right, Dick. It's just food. I expect the other boxes are full of food as well.'

They opened one or two more boxes, but they all seemed to be full of tinned food.

'Darn!' said George in disgust. 'I thought we'd found something really exciting.'

'Come on,' said Julian. 'Let's go further along the passage and see if we find anything else.'

They set off down the dark passage, but hadn't gone very far before they came to another ledge piled with more sacks and boxes.

'Wow!' exclaimed Dick. 'I bet this lot are stolen goods. Let's have a look.'

Go to **217**.

Once back in the cave, they found a sandy corner and made themselves as comfortable as possible. Anne cut some bread and butter, and made sandwiches with some of Mrs Mackie's ham. Then they each had a slice of cake, and Anne had also put in a few plums.

'That's better,' said Dick, when they had finished. 'Now – what are we going to do?'

'I've been thinking,' said Julian. 'The passage we came along from the entrance hole runs more or less straight back into the hill, doesn't it? This cave is above it, and seems to run even further back. Now, it seems to me that we can either try and find a way out by looking *up* – in the roof of the tunnel, perhaps – or we could try and find our way straight *through* the hill, and come out the other side. What do you think?'

'It would be difficult to try and find our way right through the hill,' said George doubtfully. 'After all, the passages and caves might extend for miles, like potholes. We could easily get completely lost, and that would be the end of us!'

Julian grinned at George.

'We've had plenty of experience exploring tunnels, though, haven't we,' he said. 'I've got a penknife in my pocket. We can scratch some arrows on the walls as we go, to mark our route.'

'Which way shall we go?' asked Ned. 'Back into the entrance tunnel, or along past the treasure to the cave with the stream in it?'

*If you think they should go back to the entrance tunnel, go to **234**.*

*If you think they should go past the treasure, go to **239**.*

230

*If you have arrived from **233**, score* ⌀ ⌀ ⌀ ⌀.

Julian shone his torch up the tunnel.

'Look, the tunnel goes on. Let's explore a little

further,' he said.

The others all wanted to see where the tunnel led, so they set off, Julian leading the way. The tunnel came out into another cave, not nearly as big as the one they had left behind. At one end something gleamed like silver, and seemed to move. There was a curious sound there, too.

'What is it?' asked Anne, alarmed. They stood and listened.

'Water!' said Julian suddenly. 'Of course! Can't you hear it flowing along? It's an underground stream, flowing through the hill to find an opening where it can rush out.'

'Just like that stream we saw before we came to our camping place,' said George. 'It rushed out of the hill. Do you remember? This may be the very one.'

'I'll bet it is,' said Dick. They went over to it and watched it. It rushed along in its own hollowed-out channel, close to the side of the cave wall.

Go to **226**.

231

'What, in the daylight, with any of the farm men about to see us!' said Lou with a sneer. 'Clever, aren't you.'

'Well, have you got a better idea?' asked Dan.

'Why not follow our plan?' said Lou. 'Go down when it's dark and collect the stuff. We can bring our wagon up as we planned to do tonight. We don't need to bother about forcing the children to go now – they're underground, and we can make them prisoners till we're ready to clear off.'

'I see,' grinned Dan. 'Yes – we'll close up the hole and run the caravan back over it – and come tonight in the dark with the wagon – go down and collect everything – and shut up the hole again with the children in it. We'll send a card to Giorgio when we're safe and tell him to go up and set the kids free. They won't starve. We'll leave 'em some food.'

'Right then,' agreed Lou. 'Come on, let's get that caravan over the hole so them kids are trapped.'

They ran the caravan back into place, and had a look at Pongo. He was still lying on his side, and they could see that he had a nasty wound on his head.

'Serves him right!' said Dan. 'I never could stand that chimp.'

They went away down the track.

Go to **238**.

If you have arrived from **234,** *score* ᑫ ᑫ ᑫ .
If you have arrived from **236,** *score* ᑫ ᑫ ᑫ ᑫ
ᑫ .

'Let's try and move the caravan,' said George. 'We might be able to shift it just enough.'

They all stood at the entrance hole and stared up at the planks. Julian moved some of the planks to one side, then they did their best to push at the base of the caravan with their hands, but it was no good at all.

'Perhaps Pongo can help,' Ned said suddenly. He shouted loudly: 'Pongo! Pongo, come and help!'

Everyone stood still, hoping that they would hear Pongo chattering somewhere near, but there was no sound. Poor Ned felt very worried.

'I wish I knew what's happened,' he said. 'I feel as if something terrible has happened to poor old Pongo. Where can he be?'

In fact, Pongo was not very far away. He was lying on his side, his head bleeding. He was unconscious, and could not hear the frantic calls of the children. Poor Pongo!

Go to **235**.

233

'You two were quick,' said Ned. 'Are the police coming?'

'No,' said Julian, 'we didn't get that far. Pongo broke loose from his rope and followed us down the hill, and while we were tying him up again we heard voices, and thought it might be Dan and Lou. It seemed best to come back here.'

Though neither Julian nor Anne knew it, the voices they had heard belonged to two of Farmer Mackie's men, not Dan and Lou.

'Do you think we ought to have something to eat now?' Dick asked hopefully.

'Not yet!' said George. 'We ought to decide what we are going to do next.'

Go to **230**.

234

'It would be a good idea to start by going back to the tunnel with the entrance hole,' said Dick. 'If we do find another way out, we'll be near the caravans.'

'Good idea!' agreed the others, so they made their way back down to the tunnel. Julian told them all to turn their torches on again, and as they walked along they shone them over the roof, the walls and the floor, but they could see no sign of another entrance. The walls, floor and ceiling were all formed of smooth rock.

'Oh, bother!' said Dick, after they had all had a good look. 'What shall we do now? We've got to try and get out of this rotten tunnel before it gets dark.'

Go to **232**.

<h2 style="text-align:center">235</h2>

What Julian had feared had actually happened. Lou and Dan had come back up the hill, hoping to bribe or force Ned into going back to the circus with them. When they had come near the hollow, they had stood and called loudly.

'Ned! Ned! We've come to make friends again, not to hurt you. Be a sensible boy and come back to the camp with us. Mr Giorgio is asking for you.'

When there had been no reply at all, the two men had gone nearer. Then they had seen Pongo and stopped. The chimpanzee could not get at them because he was tied up, but he sat there snarling.

'Where have those kids gone?' asked Lou.

Then he saw that the caravan had been moved back a little, and he guessed at once what had happened.

'They've found the way underground! The interfering little brutes! See, they've moved one of the caravans off the hole. What do we do *now*?'

'Deal with that dratted chimp,' said Tiger Dan in a threatening voice, and moved towards Pongo. Pongo stood up, pulling frantically at his rope to try and get away, but of course he couldn't. In his fright his foot slipped and he fell over, banging his head on a large stone. He lay quite still.

''E's dead!' exclaimed Lou.

'No, he ain't,' said Dan, 'but he won't cause us any trouble for a while. Now let's go and see if the entrance hole is open.'

They saw at once that the hole had been discovered, and that the children must have gone down it.

'They're down there now,' said Tiger Dan, almost choking with rage. 'Shall we go and deal with them – get our stuff and clear off? We meant to do it tomorrow anyway. We might as well get the stuff out now.'

Go to **231**.

236

The tunnel was so small that George could only just keep going along it. She held her torch in front of her, but she could see nothing except blackness. The air smelt damp and musty at first, but after a while it started to smell a bit fresher, and George felt a rush of excitement as she realised that there must be fresh air coming into the tunnel from somewhere. Sure enough, a moment later she saw a faint gleam of light! She squirmed forward faster and faster, and the light got brighter all the time. George could see that she was definitely coming out to the open air.

Wriggling frantically, she reached the end of the tunnel and stuck her head out of the hole – only to feel sickeningly disappointed. She had found a way out, but it came out halfway down a sheer cliff! Craning her neck upwards, she could see a bulging overhang above her, and below was a straight drop. The face of the cliff was smooth rock, like so many of the tunnels inside it, and George knew that none of them would be able to climb down it.

'Oh, blast!' she muttered, and began to crawl backwards. There was no room to turn round.

The others were all very disappointed when George got back to the cave and told them what she had found.

'Well, I think we'd better go back and collect our food and stuff from the other cave,' said Julian, 'then we can think what to do next.'

Go to **232**.

'There isn't another way out of the caves,' objected George.

'We don't know that there isn't,' said Julian thoughtfully. 'We're assuming there isn't because Dan and Lou were so keen to get us to move away from their entrance. That doesn't mean that there isn't another entrance – only that nobody's found one!'

'Well, I think we should go and have something to eat first,' said Dick. 'That will make us feel more cheerful, and then we'll plan what we're going to do. Come on, let's go back to the big cave.'

Julian made them all turn their torches off, and just use his. Not knowing how long they would be trapped underground, he didn't want to waste batteries! It was more difficult to make their way along the tunnel by the light of only one torch.

Anne walked behind Julian. She was really feeling very frightened and unhappy, and once or twice gave a little sob. Ned, who was walking behind her, gave her shoulder a little pat.

'Cheer up, Anne,' he said. 'We'll soon be out of this. Don't you worry!'

Go to **229**.

238

Not ten minutes after Lou and Dan had gone, the children came to the hole and found it blocked up. If only they hadn't stopped to explore, they would have been able to get out and set Timmy on the two men, but it was too late now. The hole was well and truly blocked. No one could get out. No one could find poor Pongo and bathe his head. They were real prisoners.

They all went back down the passage, up through the hole in the roof, and into the big cavern. Everyone felt very down and miserable, so Julian suggested that they had something to eat.

'I'm so thirsty!' exclaimed Ned.

'So am I,' said Dick. 'We could go and get a drink from that stream in the other cave. It looked quite clear and clean.'

'Good idea,' said Julian.

When they reached the stream in the other cave they dipped in their hands and drank thirstily. The water tasted lovely – so cold and clear.

'I wonder if this stream *does* go to that hole in the hillside, and pours out there,' said Julian suddenly. 'If it does, and we could follow it, we might be able to squeeze out.'

He shone his torch where the stream disappeared into a tunnel rather like the dry one they had come along.

'We could wade along, I think,' he said. 'It's fast, but not very deep. I know – I'll go along and see where it goes, and come back and tell you.'

'I think we should all go,' said George. 'You might get separated from us.'

If you think Julian should go on his own, go to **244**.
If you think they should all go, go to **249**.

'Let's go on,' suggested George. 'After all, the tunnel that leads to the entrance is made of very smooth rock – I don't think we stand much chance of finding another opening in that!'

They tidied away the remains of their picnic, and then climbed back through the hole in the cave wall and back along the passage where the treasure was stacked, then into the cave that had the stream running along the end of it.

'We'll spread out, turn our torches on, and search this cave thoroughly,' said Julian. 'Shout out if you find anything!'

George and Timmy went off together to one side of the cave. Timmy ran about, sniffing all the strange smells, while George swung her torch slowly and carefully along the walls and roof. She was so busy looking at the roof of the cave that it took her some time to notice that Timmy was scrabbling at a mound of fallen rocks at the base of the cave wall.

'What's that, Timmy?' said George, when she noticed what he was doing. 'Have you found anything?'

She bent down to take a closer look at the pile of rocks and earth. Timmy had pulled a lot of stuff loose, and George could see something that looked like a gap in the wall of the cave.

She straightened up and gave a shout.

'Hey, you lot! Come and look at this!'

Go to **242**.

240

'Perhaps I'm getting to where the stream pours out of the hill,' said Julian to himself.

He was! Some distance ahead of him, Julian suddenly saw a dim light, and wondered what it could be. He soon knew! It was daylight creeping in through the water that poured out of the hole in the hillside – poured out in a torrent into the sunshine.

With a light heart he waded along in the water. Now he would soon be out in the warm sunshine. He would let the others out, and they would race down the hill in the warmth, catch the first bus that came along, and go straight to the police.

But nothing like that happened at all.

Go to **246**.

241

If you have arrived from **246**, *score* ⌇ ⌇ .

The children ran round and round the cave, pretending to race each other, trying to get warm. They did get warm in the end, and sank down in a heap on some soft sand in a corner, panting. They sat there for a little while, trying to get their breath.

Then they heard something. Timmy heard it first and growled.

'Jumping Jiminy, what's the matter with Timmy?' said Ned in fright. He was the most nervous of the children, because he was so afraid of Dan and Lou.

They all listened, George with her hand on Timmy's collar. He growled again, softly. The noise they all heard was a loud panting, coming from the stream over at the other side of the cave!

'Someone is wading up the stream,' whispered Dick in astonishment. 'Did they get in at the place where we couldn't get out? They must have!'

'But who is it?' asked Julian. 'Can't be Dan or Lou. They wouldn't come that way when they could come the right way. Whoever it is, is arriving in the cave. I'll shut off my torch.'

Darkness fell in the cave as the light from Julian's torch was clicked off. They all sat and listened, and poor Ned shook and shivered. Timmy didn't growl any more, which was surprising. He even wagged his tail.

There was a sneeze from the other end of the cave

– and then soft footsteps padded towards them. Anne felt as if she must scream. WHO was it?

Go to **248**.

Go to **248**.

242

The other four all came running.

'Look what clever Timmy has found!' George exclaimed. 'It looks like a hole. Come on, let's see if we can move some of these rocks so that we can see it more clearly.'

The five children set to work moving the small rocks. Timmy did his best to help by scrabbling away at the little mound as well. It was slow work, because they had nothing to dig with except their hands, but eventually they had cleared most of the debris, and could see that there was a very small gap in the cave wall. Julian lay down flat on his stomach and shone his torch into the hole.

'Can you see anything, Julian?' asked Dick excitedly.

'Well, it looks as though there's a tunnel or something,' answered Julian, 'but it's so small that I can't get into it – George, I think you'd better be the one to try and crawl down it.'

'OK,' said George. 'You'd better hang on to Timmy, Julian, or he might try and follow me.'

'Good idea,' said Dick, taking a firm hold on Timmy's collar. 'Got your torch, George?'

George nodded. Then she lay down on her stomach and wriggled into the hole.

Go to **236**.

243

'Look everyone,' said Dick suddenly. 'I've got an idea. I don't know if it will work – but it really is an idea.'

'What?' asked everyone, thrilled.

'Well – what about tying a letter round Pongo's neck and sending him out of the hole again, to take the letter to the camp?' suggested Dick. 'He won't go to Dan or Lou because he's scared of them, but he'd go to any of the others all right, wouldn't he? Larry would be the best one. He seems a good fellow.'

'Would Pongo be able to do all that, Ned?' asked Julian doubtfully.

Ned looked thoughtful.

If you think Ned says Pongo can try to take a message, go to **250**.

If you think Ned says it's no use, go to **255**.

244

'No,' said Julian firmly. 'I don't think there's any point in all of us getting wet. You lot stay here, and I'll explore.'

He waded into the stream. The current tugged at

his legs, for the water ran very fast. It was only just above his knees there. He waded along by the light of the torch, wondering where the tunnel would lead.

There was a narrow ledge running beside the water, and Julian jumped up on to it. He had to crouch down as he walked because his head touched the roof of the tunnel if he didn't – but at least his legs were out of the icy cold water. Where the ledge ran beside the stream he walked along it, but at times it disappeared, and he had to wade in the water again, which had suddenly got deeper. It started to flow faster, too, and Julian realised that he was going down hill.

Go to **240**.

245

The note said:

> *'To whoever gets this note – please come up the hill to*

the hollow where there are two caravans. Under the red one is the entrance to an underground passage. We are prisoners inside the hill. Please rescue us soon.

'Julian, Dick, George, Anne and Ned.'

He read it out to the others. Then he tied the note round Pongo's neck. Pongo was surprised, but fortunately didn't try to pull it off.

'Now, you give him his orders,' said Dick to Ned. So Ned spoke slowly and importantly to the listening chimpanzee.

'Where's Larry? Go to Larry, Pongo. Fetch Larry. Go. GO!'

Pongo blinked at him and made a funny little noise as if he was saying: 'Please Ned, I don't want to go.'

Ned repeated everything again. 'Understand, Pongo? I think you do. GO, then. GO! GO!'

Pongo stood and looked at the children. He could see that they wanted him to do something important, but he was not sure that he wanted to go off on his own.

If you think Pongo goes off with the note, go to **251**.

If you think he hasn't understood, go to **257**.

246

To Julian's enormous disappointment the water got far too deep to wade through, and he stopped in fright.

'I'd better not go any further,' he said to himself. 'I could easily get swept off my feet, and the water might throw me against the side of the tunnel and I could really hurt myself. It's too sickening for words, but I think I shall have to go back to the others and tell them that this won't work.'

He felt very disappointed as he made his way back up the tunnel. He was wet and cold, too. The others questioned him eagerly as he climbed back into the cave.

'Did you find a way to get out?' asked George and Anne together.

Julian shook his head.

'It's no good,' he said. 'The stream *does* come out on the hill, but the water flows so fast, and is so deep, that we couldn't get through it. It isn't safe.'

The other four were shattered.

'Cheer up!' said Julian. 'I'm sure we'll find a way out of here somehow. Come on, let's run around and get warm. I'm frozen.'

Go to **241**.

247

It was dull after a time, sitting in the light of one torch, for they dared not use them all. Already it seemed as if Julian's torch was getting a little dim. They played all the games they could think of, and then yawned.

'What's the time? I suppose it must be getting dark outside now. I feel sleepy,' said George.

'It's nine o'clock almost,' said Julian. 'I hope Pongo has got down to the camp all right and found someone. We could expect help quite soon, if so.'

'Well, then, we'd better get along to the passage that leads to the hole,' said Dick, getting up. 'If Larry or anyone else comes, they might not be able to find us.'

They all made their way down the tunnel that led past the hidden store of valuables, and came out into the enormous cave. There was a nice sandy corner just by the hole that led down to the entrance tunnel, and the children decided to sit there and wait. They cuddled up together for warmth, feeling rather hungry.

Go to **253**.

248

Julian switched on his torch suddenly, and its light fell on a squat, hairy figure, halting in the bright glare. It was Pongo!

'*Pongo!*' everyone yelled, and leapt up at once.

Timmy ran over to the surprised chimp and sniffed round him in delight. Pongo put his arms round Ned and Anne.

'Pongo! You've escaped! You must have bitten through your rope,' said Julian. 'How clever you are to find your way through that hole where the stream pours out! How did you know you would find us here? *Clever* Pongo!' Then he saw the big wound on Pongo's head. 'Oh, look! He's been hurt. I wonder what happened? Poor old Pongo!'

'Let's bathe his head,' suggested Anne. 'I'll use my hanky.'

But Pongo wouldn't let anyone touch his wound, not even Ned. He didn't snap or snarl at them, but simply held their hands away from him, so nobody could bathe his head or bind it up.

'Never mind,' said Ned at last. 'Animals' wounds often heal up very quickly without any attention at all. He won't let us touch it, that's certain.'

Go to **243**.

'Perhaps you're right, George,' replied Julian. 'I just didn't think there was any point in us all getting wet, that's all.'

One by one they waded into the stream. The current tugged at their legs, for the water ran very fast. It got deeper and deeper as they waded along by the light of their torches, wondering where the tunnel would lead. Timmy half waded, half swam.

He didn't like this water business very much. Neither did Ned. As the water got deeper and deeper, he became frightened. He couldn't swim as well as all the others, who were used to swimming regularly at school.

'I'm scared,' he called to Julian. 'I'm almost off my feet now.'

'Me too,' said Anne.

'I think we'd better go back,' decided Julian. 'I, can see that the stream does come out on the hill, but we can't go any further – it really isn't safe. We might get knocked off our feet by the current and crack our heads on the walls of the tunnel.'

With heavy hearts they made their way back to the cave.

'Cheer up,' said Julian. 'We'll get out of here somehow, you wait and see. Come on, let's run around to warm ourselves up.'

Go to **241**.

250

*If you have arrived from **255**, score ⌂.*

'We could try him,' said Ned doubtfully. 'I do send him here and there sometimes, just for fun – to take the elephant's bat to Larry, for instance, or to put my coat away in my caravan.'

'Well, let's have a go,' said Dick. 'I've got a notebook and a pencil. I'll write a note and wrap it up in another sheet of paper, pin it together and tie it round Pongo's neck with a bit of string.'

So he wrote a note.

*Go to **245**.*

251

*If you have arrived from **257**, score ⌂.*

Suddenly Pongo turned and went! He disappeared

into the stream, splashing along by himself. The children watched him as far as they could by the light of their torches.

'He really is clever,' said Anne. 'He didn't want to go, did he? Oh, I do hope he finds Larry, and that Larry sees the note and reads it and sends someone to rescue us.'

'I hope the note doesn't get all soaked and pulpy in the water,' said Julian rather gloomily. 'I wish I wasn't so cold. Let's run round a bit again, and then have a piece of chocolate.'

They ran about and played for a time till they all felt warm again. Then they sat down and ate some chocolate, and played a guessing game to while away the time. Timmy sat close to Julian, and the boy was very glad.

'He's like a big hot-water bottle,' he said. 'Sit closer, Timmy! You'll soon warm me up!'

Go to **247**.

Anne pulled her torch out of the pocket of her jeans and turned it on. She swept the beam of light round the floor, looking for the gun that Lou had dropped. The torch lit up the panting, heaving men struggling with the children and Timmy.

'Go on, Anne!' shouted Julian. 'Do hurry up!'

Anne searched frantically round the rocky floor of the passage for the gun. At last she saw it, lying a few metres away, and she pounced on it swiftly.

'Got it!' she yelled triumphantly.

'You give that back!' shouted Dan, panting, but still unable to break away from Ned, George and Timmy. Ned was really enjoying getting his own back on the two men who had made his life a misery for so long.

Anne dodged round the struggling figures, trying to find an opportunity to hand the gun to Julian, but it was very difficult, because there were so many arms and legs and heads bobbing about in the narrow passage.

Go to **260**.

253

Anne and Ned dozed off to sleep. George almost fell asleep, too. The boys and Timmy stayed awake, and talked in low voices. At least, Timmy wagged his tail from time to time as if in agreement.

Suddenly, after what seemed like a very long time, Timmy growled, and the two boys sat up straight. Whatever it was that Timmy's sharp ears had heard, the boys had heard nothing at all. They continued to hear nothing, but Timmy kept on growling.

Julian shook the others awake.

'I think help has come,' he said, 'but we'd better not go and see, just in case it's Dan and Lou come back. So wake up and look lively!'

They were all wide awake at once. Was it Larry

come in answer to their note – or was it Tiger Dan and Lou the acrobat?

They soon knew!

Go to **258**.

254

In the cave there was a tremendous fight going on, for Pongo appeared to have got hold of both men at once. Their torches were out, and Lou didn't dare to shoot for fear of hurting Dan. Dick could see very little of this; he could only hear snarling and shouting. He tiptoed past the heaving heap on the floor with his heart in his mouth. Would they see him, and try to stop him, or would he get away safely?

If you think they spot Dick, go to **259**.
If you think he gets past safely, go to **267**.

'I really don't think Pongo could do it,' said Ned at last. 'He's quite clever, but he's only a chimpanzee. He could easily go to Dan or Lou, and then we'd be in worse trouble!'

'You don't think Pongo would go anywhere near those two, do you?' asked Anne in a horrified voice. 'We know he's afraid of them. He'd run away, wouldn't he?'

'I think he would,' agreed. 'It's just that I'm really scared of him getting into the wrong hands. He means a lot to me, does Pongo.'

The other children all felt sorry for Ned. Imagine having to depend on a chimpanzee, even one as nice as Pongo, for friendship!

'Look, Ned,' said Julian. 'I know you're worried about what might happen to old Pongo, but we've got to get out of here somehow, and he might be able to help us. I don't think he'll go anywhere near Dan and Lou – he's too scared of them. Why don't we try it?'

'Yes, Ned, let's,' said Dick.

Go to **250**.

256

Julian made up his mind. He pretended to stumble, and dropped to one knee. As he had hoped, Lou walked straight into him, with a startled yell.

'Ouch!' he shouted. 'Don't you mess around, my lad!'

'Get up!' ordered Dan.

Julian got slowly to his feet. As he did so, he cannoned back into Lou, knocking the revolver out of his hand!

'He's dropped his gun!' shouted Julian. 'Come on, you lot, let's get these two!'

The five children and Timmy fell on the two men, and a terrific scuffling broke out in the rocky passage. Timmy worried the men's legs, as Julian and Dick struggled with the furious Lou, while

Anne, George and Ned tried to hold on to Tiger Dan.

'Look for the gun, Anne!' panted Julian. 'If you can find his gun we'll be able to trap these two and go to the police!'

Go to **252**.

257

'Go on, Pongo,' encouraged Anne. 'You go off and find Larry. Come on, I'll help you.'

She took hold of Pongo's paw, and led him over to the stream. Unfortunately, Pongo thought that she wanted to play a game with him, and, clasping his arms round poor Anne, he waltzed her round and round the cave!

The others all laughed at the sight of Anne and Pongo dancing together. Pongo kept falling over Anne's feet, and Anne was struggling to make him stand still and let her go! He had been taught to dance by the man who had sold him to the circus, and he rather enjoyed it.

Eventually Ned stopped laughing long enough to tell Pongo again what they wanted him to do. Pongo let go of Anne and stood looking at Ned. He scratched his head a couple of times, as if still puzzled.

'Go, Pongo! GO ON!' shouted the exasperated Ned.

Go to **251**.

258

A head suddenly poked out of the hole nearby, and a torch shone on them. Timmy growled ferociously and struggled to fly at the head, but George held on firmly to his collar, thinking it might be Larry.

But it wasn't! It was Lou the acrobat, as the children knew only too well when they heard his voice. Julian shone his torch at the man.

'I hope you've enjoyed your little selves,' said Lou in a harsh voice. 'You keep that dog under control, boy, or I'll shoot him, see? I'm not standing no nonsense from that dog this time. Have a look at this 'ere gun!'

To George's horror she saw that Lou was pointing a gun at poor Timmy. She gave a shriek and flung herself in front of the dog.

'Don't you dare shoot Timmy! I'll – I'll – I'll . . .'

She couldn't think of anything bad enough to do to the man who could threaten to shoot Timmy, and she stopped, choked by tears of rage and fear. Timmy, not understanding why George would not let him deal with Lou, struggled and twisted in George's grasp.

'Timmy!' gasped George. 'Stand still – I can't hold you!'

*If you think George manages to hold on to Timmy, go to **263**.*

*If you think he gets away from her, go to **268**.*

Unluckily for Dick, as he made his way past the tangle of bodies, Lou rolled over and collided with his legs. Dick tried to run, but Lou's strong hands closed round his ankles like a vice.

'And just where do you think you're going, young chap?' said Lou. 'Trying to get away from us, were you?'

Dick started to struggle. Lou managed to hold on to him, but he was still having to try and fend off Pongo at the same time. Pongo was having a wonderful time getting his own back on Dan and Lou. He had a lot of old scores to settle.

Dick wondered whether to say anything to Pongo, but he was afraid that the chimp would recognise his voice, and be so pleased to see him that he would leave the two men alone, which was the last thing that Dick wanted just then!

Luckily for Dick, Pongo made such a ferocious dive at Lou that he let go of Dick's legs, and Dick jumped away from the heap of bodies as quickly as he could.

Go to **267**.

260

Julian could see the gun in Anne's hand as he swayed backwards and forwards, trying to hold on to the struggling Lou. Several times he tried to make a grab for it, but each time Lou struggled harder, and Julian needed both hands to hold on to him. Though he was thin and wiry, Lou was extremely strong. His arms and legs had been strengthened through years of tightrope walking and climbing.

Suddenly Lou gave a massive heave and broke away from the two boys! He pounced on poor Anne and wrenched the gun away from her. In a flash he had it pointed at the children again.

'Right,' he said, gasping for breath. 'You kids

let go of Dan, and don't you dare try any tricks like that again, or it'll be the worse for you, and that dog!'

One by one they set off back to where the stolen goods were stored. Lou made Julian walk in front of him, so that he could keep an eye on the boy. Julian stumbled along, feeling bitterly disappointed, and wondering whether it would be worth trying to trip up Lou again.

Go to **269**.

261

Down below, the two men had at last freed themselves from the angry chimpanzee. They might not have been able to do it but for Pongo's head wound, which was still making him feel ill. The chimp limped off in search of the children, and Lou started feeling about for his torch, and his gun.

He found the torch easily, but the gun was

nowhere to be seen.

'Never mind,' said Dan. 'Come on, let's get out of here before that dratted chimp comes back. We've got most of the stuff. I reckon we should leave the rest of it, and get out while we can.'

'Good idea,' said Lou, who was feeling rather shaken. 'Come on.'

They walked across to the hole that led down to the first cave. Lou kicked something as they went, and, pointing his torch at the ground, spotted his gun. He picked it up and stuffed it in his belt. Down they went, and along the passage, eager to get out into the night.

They had a terrible shock when they found that the hole was closed. Someone had put the planks back. *They* were prisoners now!

Go to **270**.

'Let's try the big one,' said Lou. 'There's no telling where those kids might be, but we've got to start somewhere.'

The two men switched on their torches and started to explore the huge cave.

'I don't think it's very likely that them kids would try and hide in here,' said Dan after a moment.

'They been down here a long time,' answered Lou. 'They could have found some tunnel leading off this cave that we don't know about. We only come down here to dump our stuff – we never explored much.'

'I suppose you're right,' said Dan grudgingly. 'Here, 'adn't we better start by working our way round the walls of the cave? That way we shouldn't miss anything.'

'Right,' grunted Lou.

Go to **272**.

If you have arrived from **268**, *score* ◯◁.

Timmy writhed and twisted to get away from George, but somehow she managed to hold on to him. Not knowing what the gun was, Timmy couldn't for the life of him think why George wouldn't let him get at his enemy – such a nice position, too, with his head poking through a hole like that. Timmy thought that he could deal with that head very quickly.

Lou climbed up into the cave, closely followed by Tiger Dan, who carried a couple of big sacks.

'Now, you kids, get up and go into that tunnel,' said Lou. 'Go on – go right ahead of us, and don't dare to stop. We've got work to do here tonight, and we're not going to have any more interference from kids like you. See?'

The children saw quite well. They began to walk towards the entrance of the tunnel. Julian, who was last in line, just in front of Lou, wondered whether it would be possible to trip Lou up, and make him drop the gun. The five of them and Timmy might be able to overpower the two villains then. He thought furiously as he made his way down the passage.

If you think Julian does trip Lou up, go to **256**.
If you think he decides not to try, go to **269**.

264

Lou gave a yell. 'There's one of them – look, over there! Come on!'

The men ran to where the stream came out of the tunnel, and Lou shone his torch up it. He saw the line of children with Julian last of all. He grabbed hold of the boy and pulled him back.

'Now look here,' Lou shouted to the others. 'I've got your friend here, and if you lot don't come out of that tunnel pretty quick, it'll be the worse for him. Understand?'

The four children still in the tunnel understood very well. With heavy hearts they all turned round and started to make their way back into the cave. Just as George was emerging, and Lou's attention was distracted because he was keeping an eye on Timmy, Julian managed to kick high in the air, and knock the torch out of Lou's hand. It flew up into the air and fell to the floor of the cave with a crash. Now there was total darkness.

'Get back into the tunnel, George, with Anne,' yelled Julian.

'Timmy! Timmy!' called George, but Timmy had other ideas!

Go to **275**.

265

Julian wished desperately that Pongo would bring help before Dan and Lou finished their business in the tunnel and went, leaving the children prisoners.

He watched Tiger Dan working quickly, packing everything, carrying it off, coming back again, and packing feverishly once more. Lou sat still with his torch and revolver, enjoying the scared faces of the girls and Ned. Julian and Dick put on a brave show which they were far from feeling.

Tiger Dan staggered away with another sackful. He hadn't been gone for more than half a minute before a shout echoed through the tunnel.

'Lou! Help! Something's attacking me! HELP!'

Lou got up and went swiftly down the tunnel.

'It's Pongo, I bet it's Pongo!' said Julian in excitement.

'Listen,' said Dick in an urgent voice. 'It may be Pongo by himself – he may not have gone back to the camp at all – he may have wandered about and at last gone down the entrance hole by the caravans, and come up behind Tiger Dan. If so, he won't have much chance because Lou just might shoot him, and then we won't be rescued. So I'm going to slip down the tunnel while there's a chance and hide in the big cave.'

'What good will that do?' asked Julian.

'Well, I may then be able to slip down into the passage that leads to the entrance hole and hop out without them seeing me,' said Dick, getting up. 'Then I can fetch help, see? You'd better all clear off somewhere and hide. Find a good place, Julian, in case the men come after you when they find one of us is gone. Go on.'

Without another word Dick began to walk down the tunnel, past the rocky shelf on which very little now remained, and then into the big cave.

Go to **254**.

266

The children stared at Ned in dismay. Of course, now Tiger Dan was under arrest there was nobody to look after Ned.

'Isn't there anyone at the circus who would look after you?' asked George. 'You said you'd like to work with horses – would Rossy take care of you?'

Nobby shook his head. 'Rossy wouldn't have me – he's got four kids of his own.'

'I know!' burst out Dick. 'Farmer Mackie! He keeps quite a few horses still, and his children have grown up and left home. I heard Mrs Mackie saying the other day that she found the house too big and empty now. Let's ask them if you could live there!'

'Or you could come and live at Kirrin Cottage, by the sea,' said George excitedly. 'I'm sure my mother would say yes!'

Ned looked quite perplexed. He didn't know which suggestion was the best.

If you think Ned should choose the Mackies' farm, go to **277**.
If you think he should choose Kirrin Cottage, go to **273**.

267

If you have arrived from **259**, *score* .

Dick made his way as quickly as he could in the dark to where he thought the hole was that led down into the first passage. He had to go carefully for fear of falling down it. He found it at last and let himself down into the cave below, and then, thinking it safe to switch on his torch in the passage, he flashed it in front of him to show him the way.

It wasn't long before he was out of the hole and was speeding round the caravans. Then he stopped. A thought struck him. He could fetch help all right

– but the men would be gone by then! They had laid their plans for a getaway with all their goods; there was no doubt about that.

Suppose he put the planks back over the hole, and rolled some heavy stones over the top? He couldn't move the caravan over the hole, as it was far too heavy for him, but with any luck heavy stones would do the trick. The men might think that it was the caravan overhead again.

In great excitement Dick pulled back the planks, lugging them into place, puffing and panting. Then he flashed his torch around for stones. There were several small rocks nearby. He couldn't lift them, but he managed to roll them on to the planks.

'I know I've shut the others in there with the men,' said Dick to himself, 'but I know Julian will find a good hiding place, and it won't be for long. I hope I can find my way down the hill in the darkness!'

Go to **261**.

For once, Timmy took absolutely no notice of George. He gave an enormous wriggle, and George had to let go of his collar. Timmy shot across the cave towards the place where Lou's head was sticking up.

'Timmy!' shrieked George, and flew after him.

Lou had no time to aim his gun at Timmy. He ducked down into the hole as quickly as he could, just in time to save himself from the angry dog. Timmy stood over the entrance hole, growling furiously. Lou shouted up to George.

'Here, you! Get that dog under control, and make sure you don't let go of him again. I'm coming up into that cave, and this time there'd better be no trouble, or else! Understand?'

'Yes!' shouted George sullenly.

George grabbed hold of Timmy's collar again and dragged him back to the other side of the cave. A moment later Lou's head reappeared.

Go to **263**.

269

If you have arrived from **260**, *score* ◯ ◯ ◯.

It was too risky, decided Julian. If there was a struggle, there was a real danger that the gun might go off.

The children were made to walk right past the shelf on which were the hidden goods. Then Lou sat down in the tunnel, his torch switched on fully so that he could pick out each child. He still pointed his revolver at Timmy.

'Now we'll get on,' he said to Tiger Dan. 'You know what to do. Get on with it.'

Tiger Dan began to stuff things into one of the big sacks he had been carrying. He staggered off with it, and then came back after about ten minutes and filled the other sack. It was clear that the two men meant to take everything away this time.

'Thought you'd made a very clever discovery, didn't you?' said Lou mockingly to the children. 'Oh, yes – very smart you were! See what happens to smart kids like you – you're prisoners – and here you'll stay for the next two or three days!'

'What do you mean?' cried Julian in alarm. 'Surely you wouldn't leave us here to starve?'

'Not to starve. We're too fond of you,' said Lou with a grin. 'We'll chuck you down some food, and in two or three days someone will come and rescue you.'

Go to **265**.

270

Tiger Dan went mad. One of his furious rages overtook him, and he hammered against the planks like a mad man. However, the heavy stones held them down, and the raging man dropped down beside Lou.

'Can't budge the branches! Someone must have put the caravan overhead again. We're prisoners!'

'But who's made us prisoners? Who put the branches back?' shouted Lou, almost beside himself with fury. 'We'd better go and see if those kids are still there. Come on.'

The two men went back into the tunnel, but the children were not there, of course. Julian had taken Dick's advice and found a hiding place. Dan and Lou looked at each other.

'Well, where shall we look?' said Dan. 'Shall we start in the far cave, or the big one?'

If you think they should start with the big cave, go to 262.

If you think they should try the far one, go to 278.

The policemen bundled Dan and Lou into a car, and one of them drove the wagon full of stolen goods.

'I'll come back and talk to you all tomorrow,' said the inspector. 'Look after yourselves.'

The tired children had a picnic supper, sitting on the ground and discussing the strange events of the day. Then they all fell on their bunks, fully dressed, and were sound asleep at once.

They slept very late the next morning, and hadn't finished breakfast when the inspector arrived to talk to them. They told him all about finding the entrance to the underground caves, and stumbling on the pile of stolen goods.

'Well, we're very grateful to you all,' said the inspector finally, as he got to his feet. 'We've been suspicious of those two for a long time, but we haven't been able to prove anything. Thank you all very much!'

After he had gone, the children talked about what

they were going to do that day. Ned sat very quietly, looking pale and tired.

'What's the matter, Ned?' asked Anne. 'You don't look at all happy.'

'Well,' said Ned, 'I been wondering what will happen to me now!'

Go to **266**.

272

The two men made their way over to the side of the huge cave. It was so big that it would take them a very long time to work their way all round. The phosphorescent walls shimmered and gleamed in the torchlight.

'I think I found something, Lou,' said Dan after a few minutes. 'Look!'

He shone his torch down towards the floor of the cave, and Lou could see what looked like the mouth of a small tunnel. It was so small that a grown man couldn't have got in to it, but a child could have just managed it. Lou lay down flat on his stomach and shone his torch into the tunnel.

'Can you see anything, Lou?' asked Dan.

Lou thrust his arm, holding the torch, as far into the tunnel as he could.

'No,' he said. 'There ain't nothing in there.'

He got to his feet. 'Come on,' he said. 'We got to find them kids.'

Go to **276**.

273

'You'd love Kirrin Cottage,' Anne told Ned. 'There's Aunt Fanny, who's really kind, and the beach, and George's boat, and Kirrin Island, which has a castle and a shipwreck, and – oh, everything!'

Ned's eyes were shining. 'It sounds wonderful,' he said. 'I think I'd like to live there very much indeed!'

'Oh, good!' said George, but Julian shook his head.

'It would never work,' he said. 'Just think what Uncle Quentin would have to say.' He turned to Ned. 'George's father is a scientist who does important experiments,' he explained. 'He doesn't really like having children around, most of the time.'

George hung her head.

'I suppose you're right,' she said sadly. 'Sorry, Ned. I should have thought about that. Perhaps it wasn't such a good idea after all.'

Ned looked suddenly very lost, and Anne put a hand on his arm.

Go to **277**.

274

Dan and Lou kept bumping into each other as they searched the floor of the cave. Crawling around on their hands and knees in the dark they banged their heads together two or three times, and nearly had another row with each other. However, Dan found a torch at last, and tried to turn it on.

'Drat this torch!' he exclaimed. 'It ain't working!'

'Give it a good shake,' suggested Lou.

Dan shook the torch hard a couple of times, and then turned it on. This time a beam of light flashed out into the darkness, and soon they had found the other torch as well.

'Right,' said Dan. 'We know those kids aren't in this cave. We'd better go and look somewhere else.'

Go to **278**.

275

Timmy couldn't see Lou, but he could certainly smell him! He flew at Lou, sending him crashing to the ground. Down went the man with a crash and a yell, and the revolver flew out of his hand. Julian heard it slithering across the floor of the cave, and felt very thankful.

'Put your torch on, George, quickly!' he yelled. 'We must see what we're doing. Goodness, here's Pongo now!'

Tiger Dan gave a yell of fright when the torch flashed on and he saw the chimpanzee making straight for him. He gave the ape a tremendous push, which sent him flying, then turned to run. Lou was trying frantically to fend off the excited Timmy.

Dan ran to the tunnel – and then stopped in astonishment. Four burly policeman were pushing their way out of the tunnel, led by Dick. One of them carried a revolver in his hand. Dan put his hands up at once. George called Timmy off, and he left Lou rather reluctantly. Lou got up with great difficulty. Then he saw Dick.

'So one of you kids did slip out – and shut the hole on us!' he said savagely. 'I might have guessed.'

'You hold your tongue, Lewis Allburg,' snapped

the inspector. 'You're going to have a lot of talking to do later on!'

'Dick! How did you get here so soon?' asked Julian. 'Surely you didn't go all the way to the town and back?'

'No, I went down to the farm and used the Mackies' telephone. The police arrived in double quick time,' said Dick, grinning.

The police handcuffed Dan and Lou, and then they all made their way down the tunnel, past the place where the stolen goods had been stored. The inspector collected the few things that were left. Then they made their way through the cave with the gleaming walls, down through the hole and into the small cave, and along the narrow passage to the entrance hole. Finally they climbed wearily out into the fresh air.

Go to **271**.

Dan and Lou started to move forward again in single file, but suddenly Lou, who was in the lead, tripped over a stone. He fell flat on his face on the cave floor, his torch flying from his hand. It landed some distance away, and the light went out. Dan still had his torch on, but as he bent over Lou to help him up, Lou sat up suddenly, knocking his head against Dan's arm. Dan dropped his torch too! The cave was plunged into darkness.

'Now look what you done!' yelled Lou in a fury. 'We'll have to find both those torches before we can look any further, and when we do find them, they'll probably be broken. You're a real fool, Dan!'

Dan lost his temper.

'I ain't no fool!' he shouted at Lou. 'You're the fool, tripping over like that! Now, just shut up and let's try and find the torches before the kids get away.'

The two men got down on their hands and knees and started to feel round the cave floor.

Go to **274**.

277

If you have arrived from **273**, *score* ◠.

'If you lived with the Mackies, you'd be near all your circus friends in the camp,' said Julian. 'Just think, you could see Pongo and Barker and Growler whenever you wanted!'

Ned smiled. 'I don't think I could bear to be too far from the animals,' he said. 'Do you think the Mackies would have me?'

'Let's go and ask them now!' said Julian. 'We'll soon find out.'

Julian and Ned went off to the farm, and saw the Mackies.

'Why, yes,' said the farmer. 'I'd be glad to give the

boy a home. You'll have to go to school regular-like, but I'd welcome help with the horses.'

Ned grinned broadly. 'Thanks, Mr Mackie,' he said gratefully. 'You won't regret it!'

Go to **279**.

278

If you have arrived from **274***, score* ⌣ ⌣ ⌣ ⌣.

'Let's try the far cave,' said Lou. 'Come on.'

The children had gone up to the small cave, but at first there didn't seem to be anywhere to hide.

'I don't know where we can go,' said Julian, feeling rather desperate. 'It's no good wading down that stream again – we'll only get cold and wet, and we won't be able to escape from there if the men come after us!'

'I can hear something,' said George suddenly.

'Put your light out, Julian – quickly!'

The torch was snapped off, and the children waited in darkness. Timmy didn't growl, and George could feel that he was wagging his tail.

'I think it might be Pongo,' whispered George to the others. 'Put the torch on again.'

The light flashed out, and picked out the chimpanzee, who was coming towards them across the cave.

'He hasn't been down to the camp, unfortunately,' said Julian. 'Look, the note is still round his neck. Darn! Now, where are we going to hide?'

'Up the stream,' said Anne suddenly. 'We've tried going down it, but we haven't tried going up it. Do you think it would be any good?'

'Let's try it,' said Julian. 'I can't think of anything else!'

Ned went first, stepping on to the narrow ledge inside the rocky tunnel, just above the rushing water. He was followed by Pongo, then Anne, George, Timmy – and last of all, Julian.

But just as Julian was disappearing, the two men

came into the cave, and by chance Lou's torch shone right on to the vanishing boy!

Go to **264**.

279

While they were at the farm, Julian took the chance to telephone his parents and tell them what had happened. His mother was horrified, and told them that they must start for home at once.

When he got back he told the others that they had to go home. They were all disappointed that their caravanning adventure was coming to an end. They said goodbye to Pongo, who was going back to the circus, where Larry would look after him. Then they said goodbye to Ned. He was sad to see his friends go, but was looking forward to his new life on the farm. The others knew that he would be properly looked after from now on.

Ned and Mr and Mrs Mackie stood on the cart

track to wave goodbye to the two caravans the next morning.

'Good luck! See you again some time, I hope!' called Ned.

'Goodbye!' shouted the four children.

'Woof! Woof!' barked Timmy, which was his way of saying goodbye to his friend Pongo.

'Well,' said Julian, as the two caravans rolled homewards, 'that was quite an adventure!'

How many red herrings have you collected?

0–25   Very good indeed! The Famous Five must have been glad to have you with them.

26–50   Promising. Perhaps your next adventure with the Famous Five will be even more successful.

51–75   You took a long time getting there, didn't you? You'll have to do better than that to keep up with the Famous Five!

More than 75 Oh, dear! Perhaps you should go back to the beginning of the story and try again.

Join the Famous Five on more of their exciting adventures.

The Famous Five Adventure
Game Book 1
based on *Five On A Treasure Island*

The Famous Five Adventure
Game Book 2
based on *Five Go Adventuring Again*

The Famous Five Adventure
Game Book 3
based on *Five Run Away Together*

The Famous Five Adventure
Game Book 4
based on *Five Go To Smuggler's Top*

The Famous Five Adventure
Game Book 6
based on *Five On Kirrin Island Again*

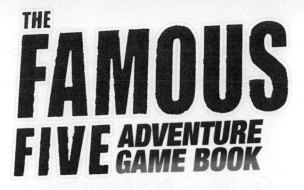

THE FAMOUS FIVE ADVENTURE GAME BOOK

Meet the Famous Five and be part of the adventure in these bumper fun game books.

Follow the clues and solve the mystery but watch out for red herrings!

For more fun and games visit www.famousfivebooks.com

Game Book 1

Game Book 2

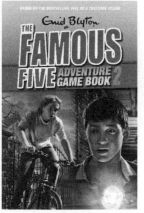

9781444900897 £4.99

9781444900903 £4.99

Meet Peter, Janet and Jack, Barbara, Pam, Colin and
George. Together they are The Secret Seven —
ready to solve any mystery, anytime!
A great introduction to adventure stories.

For the full range of Secret Seven books and eBooks, please see
www.hodderchildrens.co.uk

Hodder
Children's
Books

Elizabeth Allen is spoilt, mischievous and determined to get home — whatever the cost — she really is the Naughtiest Girl in the school! Exciting stories about the girls and boys boarding at Whyteleafe School.

THE
FAMOUS FIVE'S
SURVIVAL GUIDE

includes the NEW Unsolved Mystery

Packed with useful information on surviving outdoors and solving mysteries, here is the one mystery that the Famous Five never managed to solve. See if you can follow the trail to discover the location of the priceless Royal Dragon of Siam.

The perfect book for all fans of mystery, adventure and the Famous Five!

ISBN 9780340970836

www.famousfivebooks.com

Check out the brand new Famous Five website.

Featuring games and downloads from avatars to screen savers for mobile phones and wallpapers. Enter our amazing monthly competitions and online team challenges to win fab prizes, including limited edition merchandise only available on the website.

www.famousfivebooks.com

www.hodderchildrens.co.uk

Hodder Children's Books